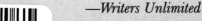

S0-CWP-882

DRIVING YOUR BOYFRIEND CRAZY

I could hear myself shrieking and didn't seem able to stop. My fingers were clenched so tight around the steering wheel of Seth's old Honda that it's amazing it didn't shatter. The thought skittered through my spazzed-out mind that I really could shatter his steering wheel, with the whole super strength thing and all.

"Jessie, if you'll just—" He was using his reasonable voice on me again. I had no time for reasonable.

"Seth! The clutch! Don't use that 'calm down, Jessie' voice on me when I'm hurtling us down a mountain in a five-thousand-pound steel instrument of death. Where's the FREAKING CLUTCH?"

"Jessie, we're going seven miles per hour over a speed bump. You've got to relax. There is no clutch, remember? This is an automatic, like we talked about? All you have to do is gently press on the—AAARGHHH!"

Other books by Jax Abbott:
SUPER *WHAT*?

SUPER 16

JAX ABBOTT

SMOOCH NEW YORK CITY

This book is dedicated to my readers.
Being a teenager—sometimes it's awesome, and
sometimes it bites, but it's almost never boring. Take
it from somebody who lived through nearly as many
hideously embarrassing moments as Jessie has:
laughter makes it so much better.
Huge hugs,
Jax

SMOOCH ®

February 2005

Published by

Dorchester Publishing Co., Inc.
200 Madison Avenue
New York, NY 10016

ISBN 0-8439-5407-8

Visit us on the web at www.smoochya.com.

ACKNOWLEDGMENTS

Thanks to Dr. Mary Hein, who helped me plot my evil orthodontist, and who is a fabulous dentist, in spite of that teensy over-fondness for drilling.

Thanks also to my wonderful editor, Kate Seaver, who understood when a crisis caused a missed deadline. Oh, and for the chocolate. Much, lovely chocolate. Thanks!!

Thanks to Kresley Cole, who took time out of her own deadline to reassure me I wasn't sucking all humor out of the ozone with my writing, and to Beverly Brandt, who helped me through the Bad Time, and to Lani Diane Rich and Michelle Cunnah, who made me laugh when nothing else was funny.

Thanks most of all to my wonderful husband, Judd, who always gives me the bigger bowl of ice cream, and who told me I had big, smelly feet when I needed to laugh, and to Connor and Lauren, who are my reason for everything.

-1-

COUNTDOWN TO SUPER 16

"There's no way I'm going to the orthodontist. My teeth look fine." I peered into the mirror with my lips scrunched as far back from my pearly whites as they could go. I mean, sure, they weren't, like, perfect Hollywood teeth, but who wants to work that hard? And really, some of those stars were going way too far with this new whitening trend, if you asked me. Who wanted glow-in-the-dark teeth? Especially down here in Florida, where it would just make it easier for the alligators to find you at night when you screamed.

"Yes, you are going to the orthodontist." My mom had her "poor me, I should have had a Pet Rock instead of daughters" expression on her face as she brought clean towels into the bathroom and opened the linen cupboard. "The dentist said you might have a problem with your jaw being a little narrow and it wouldn't hurt to get it checked out. That doesn't automatically mean you're going to need braces, Jess."

She turned around and looked at me in the mirror as she sent the towels floating to their proper place on the shelves behind her.

"Oh, right. The behind-the-back towel-sorting trick. You telekinetics are such show-offs," I muttered.

Mom just laughed and hugged me. "That's me. A big show-off. So the show-off's daughter needs to get ready to go to the orthodontist. Five minutes, kiddo."

The final towels in place, she glanced at the cupboard and the doors swung shut as she left the room. I grinned. For two years there hadn't been much laughing or hugging from Mom, as she tried to get over how devastated she was that Dad died. So it felt good, but was a little weird, kind of like when you get a new pillow because your old one was squooshed flat, and the new one feels great but doesn't smell just right yet.

Not that moms are pillows, but you know what I mean.

"Jessie's getting braces. Jessie's getting braaa-ayces." The biggest annoyance in my life, otherwise known as my baby sister, Chloe, skipped into the bathroom. "Hey, metal mouth, taking a last look at your teeth before they look like railroad tracks? Bet Seth won't want to kiss you then."

She giggled and danced away from me, hair flying, when I tried to swat her. Chloe was blessed with the good hair genes in the family—Mom's straight, silky blond. It didn't help endear her to me, you understand. Of course, she also got Mom's telekinetic powers, so there must be something to that whole genetics concept.

She grabbed the hand towel and clutched it to her, then started making fake kissing sounds and talking in a bizarre, high-pitched voice. "Oh, mwah, mwah, mwah. Oh, Jessie, you are the love of my life, you—*Ow!* My lips are stuck in your braces! Ouch! Ow! Ouch!"

"Get *out*, monster, before I use my super-strength and squish you like a bug."

Sadly, empty threats didn't work on Chloe. She stuck her tongue out at me.

"Girls! Get down here right now."

I sighed and grabbed my hairbrush so I could try to detangle the Mop of Doom in the car. After all, "jaw a little narrow" didn't mean I definitely needed braces, right? Not with my sixteenth birthday only twelve days, eleven hours, and seventeen seconds away?

No way could Fate be so cruel after the past few months I've had.

- 2 -

FATE IS A MEAN BEEYOTCH

"You've got to have braces." The woman leaning over me had a face like a porcelain doll, except for the glowing red eyes. Okay, her eyes didn't actually glow, but there was definitely an evil demon inside her somewhere. I mean, her name was actually Dr. Payne—how sick and twisted is that?

I yanked my jaw away from the iron grip of her gloved fingers. "Whagg ooo eeen, ayces?"

She looked at me blankly.

Oh, right.

I spat the wads of cotton out of my mouth.

7

"What do you mean, braces? My dentist said I just had a slightly narrow jaw. What part of that means I have to get braces? My teeth aren't crooked. Trust me, I can categorize every single physical flaw I have in two minutes and twelve seconds flat—there are eighty-five—and crooked teeth isn't one of them. Now, if you'd mentioned that my tongue is slightly odd-shaped, I'd go along with you. That's number forty-seven. But braces? No way."

I was huddled so far back in the corner of the plastic-covered dental chair, I could feel the imprint of the arm in my back.

Her "I'm a professional; you can trust me with your child" face she'd worn for Mom's benefit dropped off, now that Mom was out in the waiting room.

"Look, kid, don't give me any crap. My old drill broke down on me, and I have to wait three days for the new one. Three whole days." She stared off into space, a crazed gleam in her eyes, while fondling the enormous metal contraption hooked up next to the chair.

Suddenly her gaze snapped back to me. "You need braces, and you need a jaw spreader. We could just break your jaw to open it up, if you like. They do that, you know. Of course, it never heals right, and you'll be freakishly deformed for the rest of your life, but if you want to look

8

like a teenage reject from *National Geographic* magazine, go for it."

She pointed a long, bony finger right in my face. "Just don't say I never warned you."

Then, right there in front of me, she did the Jekyll-Hyde thing. She closed her eyes and took a deep breath. When she opened her eyes, Psycho Demon Dentist was gone and the person my mother had met was back.

She opened the door and called to a waiting dental assistant, "Will you please call in Mrs. Drummond, so we can have a consultation? You can take Jessie back out to the waiting room. Thank you."

I cringed past her, expecting her evil alternate personality to show up at any second and come after me with the drill. Talk about your wack jobs. *Wait till I tell Mom about this.*

"What do you mean, you really like her? She's a nutcase! She told me she'd break my jaw, and I'd be in *National Geographic*. You didn't fall for her Dr. Jekyll side, did you?" I stared at my clueless mother in disbelief. "You know, no disrespect, but I think dating has frazzed your brain, Mom. There's no way I'm going back to that dentist."

Mom pulled the car into the driveway and slammed it into park unnecessarily roughly, I thought, from my lofty perspective of having one whole driving lesson under my belt. (Well, only the classroom part, not the behind-the-wheel part, but still.)

"Jessie, we've had this discussion the entire drive home. I'm tired of it. I'm sorry you hate the idea, but Dr. Payne—who seems like a lovely person to me—says you need braces. You're set for an appointment for the impressions later this week, and she'll put them on next Friday. End of discussion."

My eyes bugged out. I could feel it; I could imagine how gross it must look, but I was beyond caring.

"*Next Friday?* That's the day before my birthday! Are you nuts?" said my bug-eyed self.

Mom paused in opening the car door and sighed. "Yes, I know. I'm sorry, honey, but that's the only day she had available in the next two months. It's better to get it done and over with, don't you think? Is there something in your eye?"

As she climbed out of the VW, I fell back against the seat, mouth hanging open. *Great. Just great. My life is over.*

"Your life is over," Lily, one of my mondo best (in spite of her long legs, silky blond hair, and Ph.D.-level vocabulary) friends, announced, while she hung over the side of my bed examining her freshly painted toenails. "I mean, no offense, Jess, but with the frizzy-hair thing and the braces, you're going to turn into a caricature of a funny-looking teenager. We're totally going to have to get you a different hairdo."

Only a really good friend could get away with saying something like this. But still . . . "Thanks, Lily. I'm *so* glad you came over to cheer me up. I feel so much better now, I may just gouge my eyes out." I pulled my pillow over my head and moaned, then did a mental backtrack and peeked out. "And what's a caricature?"

"It's like a cartoon that exaggerates character traits. And quit moaning. *I'm* the drama queen in this group," said my other best (in spite of looking like a teenage Halle Berry) friend, Avielle, from her perch on my red comfy chair in the corner. "Look, this month's *Cosmo Girl* has trendy short haircuts you can get with curly hair. If we cut your hair almost all off, everybody will be so freaked by the hair, they'll hardly notice the braces."

I pulled the pillow all the way off of my face and moaned louder. "Again with the *not* helpful. Look, if this is the best you two can come up with, maybe you should just leave me alone with my misery."

11

I studied my friends. (Note to self for future: try *not* to find friends who are so much more beautiful than self.)

Lily rolled over and sat up, her long legs stretched out in front of her beneath her pink denim mini. "Translation: Jessie wants to call Seth and get some sympathy. 'Oh, poor Jessie. Let me come over and kiss it all better.'" She giggled.

I threw the pillow at her. "Like you can talk about kissing, Miss Wears a Hickey to the Football Game. Tough tutoring session with John, was it?"

Lily blushed. "Well, it's kind of positive reinforcement when he figures something out in his homework. It's been proven by cognitive behaviorists that—"

"Puh-*leeeze!*" Avielle rolled her eyes. "Save the five-dollar words for somebody you can bamboozle, girlfriend. You're making up on all the kissy-face you missed while John was off living with his parents. Now that he's home, you're so lovey-dovey it's sickening."

Lily's face turned even redder. "Okay, okay. There may be some making up for lost time going on. But he was gone for two months. And if it had been up to evil Kelli, he'd still be gone. I swear, I need to get revenge on that girl."

We all grinned as we thought back to how we'd foiled Kelli's sabotage of the Harvest Prom king and queen voting so Lily's boyfriend could be elected king. (His former homecoming-queen mother was big on that sort of thing, so she'd let him move back to Skyville to live with his extended family and finish out high school. Long story; great ending.)

I jumped up to find another color of nail polish; Mosh Pit Mauve was *so* last week. My nail polishes were all in a bin on my dresser right under my beloved Orlando Bloom poster. I couldn't decide which was better—Orli as a tortured, sensitive elf in *Lord of the Rings,* or as a tortured, sensitive soul in *Troy,* or as a tortured, sensitive swashbuckler in *Pirates.* The man just did tortured and sensitive really well.

Avielle snickered. "Quit drooling over that poster and pay attention, Jess. Anyway, does Seth know how much time you spend staring into Orli's *tortured, sensitive* eyes?"

I sighed and turned around. My so-called friends were cracking up. "That's the last time I share the innermost workings of my soul with you two oafs. And no, I don't exactly mention Orli to Seth."

Avielle sat up straighter and clasped her hands in her lap. If you can look serious in a yel-

low sparkly T-shirt that says I AM TOTALLY ALL THAT, she looked serious.

"Okay, let's get to why I called this meeting."

I looked at Lily. "This is a meeting? I thought we were hanging out to do manis and pedis and gorge on large amounts of pizza and diet Coke. Should I take notes or something?"

"Yes, you should take notes on the kind of pizza we want. Thin and crispy with extra cheese and pepperoni and mushrooms but no onions, please." Lily of the supermodel-thin body always ate more than the rest of us put together. How unfair is that?

Avielle wasn't smiling. "Hey, I'm serious, guys. Talk now; pizza later. We have a problem."

I sank back down on the edge of the bed. "What is it this time? Haven't we had enough disasters to deal with?"

If they only knew about the disasters I've had to deal with lately. But the League frowns upon telling Normals about the existence of superheroes. Even if the Normals are their best friends.

Avielle looked down at the carpet. "It's like this. You know how Mike dumped Kelli at the prom, after she tried to rig the ballot box? So now she's guyless for the first time in her nasty little life?"

Lily and I nodded. Mike Brooklyn was the poster child for high school yum. He was the tall blond-haired, blue-eyed, football team quarterback and captain, and he hadn't appreciated Kelli's attempts to block his best player's return to the team. His and head cheerleader Kelli's long-running on-again, off-again relationship had exploded that night.

Kind of like my brain when I saw Mom kissing Sheriff Luke. But that, as they say down here in Florida, is a "whole 'nuther story."

Avielle drew in a deep breath. "I'm sorry, Lily, but I think she's after John now."

"What? *My* John?" Lily looked stunned. For somebody with an Einstein-level IQ, she always found the plottings of evil cheerleaders oddly shocking.

Avielle nodded, eyes narrowed and jaw clenched. "I heard her talking to her evil minions, as Jessie calls them, in the gym after school. I was up on the stage behind some of the set scenery, painting, and they must not have seen me. Now that John has college scouts after him and got that write-up in the *Skyville Gazette,* she feels that he's suddenly 'worthy' of her. The evil witch."

Lily sat there, gaping. "I . . . you . . . *what?* She's going to go after *John?* But she can't . . .

he won't . . . he's just not sophisticated enough to deal with her. What am I going to do?"

I put an arm around her shoulders and hugged. "Hey, no sweat. John loves you. He's not only the size of a mountain; he's got a heart that big. He's not going to fall for her crap. Heck, he can't even see any other girls when you're in the room."

Lily jerked away from me and stood up. "That's just it. *When I'm in the room.* What about the time she gets to him when I'm not around? I trust John, but Kelli is like some marauding force of ancient evil. A mere mortal doesn't stand a chance. Especially a sixteen-year-old ball of rampaging hormones."

Avielle and I looked at each other. We'd had the feeling that John was trying for second base, and maybe even more, with Lily lately, but she wouldn't talk to us about it. "Ball of rampaging hormones" sounded pretty much like we'd been right.

I stood up, too. "If 'marauding force of ancient evil' means hairy, nasty thing, I'm with you. But I still don't think we have anything to worry about, Lils. Just tell John you heard Kelli was going to be putting the moves on him. Forewarned is forearmored, and all that."

Lily hugged herself, almost shivering. "It's forearmed, Jess. And I'm not going to tell John

16

anything. I'm not going to lower myself to Kelli's level. If he loves me enough, he won't have anything to do with her. He should be able to figure it out."

Avielle shook her head. "Look, I understand what you're saying. I really do. But it sounds a lot like when Mom hates her birthday present because she expected Dad to psychically know what she wanted. Shop online and give the dude the URL, is my motto. Men are sheep. They need to be herded along."

She waved the silver charm bracelet that last month's boyfriend, the deejay, had given her. "Do you think I got this by being subtle?"

I totally want to be like Avielle when I grow up. Fearless, beautiful, and with great jewelry.

I grabbed my phone. "No use trying to figure this out on an empty stomach. Extra cheese, Lils?"

Lily looked at me with a dazed expression on her face and then blinked rapidly. She grabbed her purse and ran for the door. "Sorry, but I'm not really hungry anymore. I'll . . . um, I'll talk to you guys later."

I opened my mouth to call her back, but I could already hear her steps pounding down the stairs. I closed my mouth and turned to Avielle. "Are you staying?"

She nodded grimly. "Yeah. We need to figure out an action plan. If Lily won't fight back, I have no problem doing it for her. Extra onions."

"We're going to fight with onions?" Okaaay, this sounded fun in a bizarre kind of way. We could make Kelli smell totally nasty, and . . .

"On the *pizza*, Jess. Onions on the pizza. I swear, sometimes you are a superdork." Avielle grinned at me, probably to let me know she was just kidding.

I picked up the phone to dial for an extra-large, *half*-onion pizza, and paused.

"Oh, if you only knew, Avielle. If you only knew."

-3-

SUPERSTRENGTH IS ROMANTIC. NOT.

"Which one is the clutch? Seth. *Seth!* Which one is the *clutch?*" I could hear myself shrieking but didn't seem able to stop. My fingers were clenched so tight around the steering wheel of Seth's old Honda that it was amazing it didn't shatter. The thought skittered through my spazzed-out mind that I really could shatter his steering wheel, with the whole superstrength thing and all.

I loosened my death grip on the wheel a smidge.

"Jessie, if you'll just—" Seth was using his reasonable voice on me again. I had no time for reasonable.

"Seth! The clutch! Don't use that 'calm down, Jessie' voice on me when I'm hurtling us down a mountain in a five-thousand-pound steel instrument of death. Where's the *freaking clutch?*"

"Jessie, we're going seven miles per hour over a speed bump. You've got to relax. There is no clutch, remember? This is an automatic, like we talked about. All you have to do is gently press on the brakes—*aaarghhh!*"

I moved the little stick thing to the P position and then glared at my so-called boyfriend. "If you'd sit back in your seat properly, instead of hovering, you wouldn't get jolted by the seat belt when I stop the car, Seth Blanding."

"Jolted? Stop the car? Jessie, you slammed on the brakes so hard, the seat belt nearly took my head off! Although, on second thought, maybe this driving lesson would be easier on me if I didn't have a head. You're a menace!"

He reached over and snatched the keys out of the ignition and then got out of the car, slamming the door. Luckily we were in the Skyville High parking lot after school, so there wasn't any traffic to run him over. I expected him to stalk away, but he just bent his yummy, long, lean runner's body over and sort of gasped in these deep, shuddering breaths, his gorgeous dark-chocolate hair flopping over his forehead.

Honestly, some boys have no guts whatsoever, to get all worked up over a little driving lesson.

Well, okay. It was more like forty-five solid minutes of me shrieking in Seth's ear, to be fair. Plus, if I ever wanted him to kiss me again, I might want to be a little nicer. He *was* doing me a favor, after all. (With the driving lesson, not the kissing thing. He likes kissing me, too.)

I got out of the car, opening and closing my fingers to try to make some basic blood flow happen, and walked over to his side of the car. "Um, Seth? I'm sorry if I got a little, um, excited."

He laughed. At least, I think it was a laugh. It sounded kind of hoarse and desperate.

"A little excited? A *little* . . . Jessie, if you get that kind of *little* excited during your lessons with Mr. Platt, you're going to drive the poor man straight into cardiac arrest. No pun intended."

I narrowed my eyes. I hadn't been *that* bad. "I don't appreciate your pathetic attempts at humor, Blanding. Just because your precious algebra teacher has bad nerves, which you should expect, 'cause he's like, a hundred years old, doesn't mean—"

"Bad nerves? Jessie, he'd have to take some

kind of nerve pills to put up with you. You are the worst driver I've ever seen in my life. And that's saying a lot, here in the land of old-lady drivers."

Oh, that was *so* totally it.

"Oh, really? Well, why don't you just find another girlfriend? One who's a better driver, Mr. Know-it-all. I'm leaving. This lesson is over." I stalked off—but kinda slowly, so he could catch up and apologize—and listened for the sound of his footsteps running up behind me.

Stalking and listening for footsteps.

Stalking (a little more slowly) and listening.

Stalking (actually kind of ambling by then) and listening really hard. Superlistening by then, even.

Whew. Footsteps, finally. He scared me for a minute, there. If he'd called my bluff, then what would I do? Walk home the two miles in these shoes?

"Jessie, wait up. I'm sorry I said you were the worst driver ever. Please don't go off mad. I'm sure it's just nerves from never driving before and you'll, ah . . . you'll get the hang of it." He sounded suspiciously like he was swallowing his tongue, but he got the words out, so I considered that good enough to forgive him.

Plus there was the teensy two-mile-walk problem.

Seth caught up to me and put his hand on my arm. "Look, I have an idea. Let's go to the beach over at Manatee State Park. For five dollars you can drive out to the water and park on the beach to have a picnic. It'll give you a chance to drive in a nice, peaceful environment with beautiful scenery, and maybe you'll be a little, um, calmer."

I just looked at him. "Right, because the idea of running over small children and their sand castles is so relaxing to me. How about *you* drive out to the beach, and we have a nice, relaxing picnic, instead? We can pick up some KFC on the way."

He jumped on the idea so fast, it wasn't all that flattering.

"Great! I mean, yeah, we could do that, if you want. . . ."

I slowed to a stop and sneaked a glance at him. *Oh, not the puppy-dog eyes.* I started laughing. "That is so not fair, to do the puppy-dog eyes on me, Seth. You know I always give in when you do that."

He just grinned. The eyes in question were a deep, rich brown with little flecks of gold in them. Almost like amber, as I'd started to tell Chloe until she'd made fake gagging noises and ran around the living room, clutching her throat.

Seven-year-old girls are so immature.

Seth put his hands on my shoulders. "Jess? Are we okay?"

"We're fine. But we might want to leave the driving lessons to the professionals. You seem to have weak nerves." I turned around and made a dash for it, giggling. Seth chased after me and caught up as I reached the car.

Well, I kinda let him catch me.

"Hey, you," he said, tipping my head up with two fingers under my chin. "I kinda like you, y'know?"

"I kinda like you, too. Even if you are . . . Oh." It's hard to keep teasing a guy when he's kissing you. And he has the nicest lips. Just the right combo of firm and soft. Not squishy or drooly or chapped or anything yucky. Just perfect, actually.

Yummm.

Hooonnnnnnnnnkkkkkkkkkk!

The blare of the car horn startled us apart. It was Kelli and the cheerleader clones in her convertible, natch.

"Get out of the middle of the parking lot with your PDA, already, you two!" She sneered at us and then drove off.

Seth looked at me, confused. "Why is she talking about my Palm Pilot?"

I rolled my eyes. Sometimes I forgot what a geek I was dating. "Not personal digital assistant. Public display of affection, you goober. We really have to wean you from the frightening world of electronics and out into normal society sometime."

He started laughing. "Right, Super Babe. I forgot you know all about normal."

I grinned, but glanced around to make sure nobody'd heard. Seth was the only one of my Normal friends who knew about the existence of superheroes (and that I was one) and the League of Liberty. It's another long story, but he knew I wasn't a Normal, and he liked me anyway.

We strapped on our seat belts and headed for KFC, Seth back behind the wheel. I'd never admit it, but I wasn't all that bummed to let him drive. At least, *this* time.

"Have you heard from E lately?"

E is my crazy grandmother Elisabeth, a fearless kick-butt superhero. She has my crazy red hair (that's gorgeous on her) and lives on an island. She also has the most annoying tendency to one-up every single thing I go through.

We talked about E and rocked out to some tunes while we drove through the chicken place and ordered a meal of basically all carbs plus gravy. After growing up in Seattle, a.k.a. Tofu City, all I could think was: *Ya gotta love the South.*

"So how far is it to the beach?" I asked around a mouthful of biscuit. Mom would *so* have a table-manners cow.

"Not far. We just—"

Bang!

The car jolted as if something heavy'd smashed into us, and the front end started swerving around. My mashed potatoes up-ended over my skirt and my soda flew out of my hand and hit Seth in the head. He slammed on the brakes and skidded to a stop on the side of the road, then slammed the car into park.

"What the heck was that? Did somebody shoot us?" I jerked my head from side to side, searching for the shooter or shooters, and the words kept tumbling out of my mouth. "Seth, we need to get out and hide under the car until we can get help. Do you have your cell phone? It may be somebody who knows about my su-perpowers. Are you hit? Do we need to—"

"Jessie. Jessie! It's just a blowout. A flat tire. Nobody was shooting at us. Calm down." Seth unbuckled his seat belt and wiped dripping ice cubes out of his hair.

I whooshed out a deep breath and looked

around. Seth was right. No shooters in sight. No *anybody* in sight, in fact. (Must quit watching *Alias* so much.) We were on a long stretch of road with a whole lot of nothing in sight. I opened the door and got out, trying to push mashed potatoes off my legs.

Gravy is not my best look.

I noticed how neatly he'd managed to park the car on the side of the road and cringed, thinking of how I might have reacted if it had been me behind the wheel when we got blown out. Or when we got the blowout. I guess "blown out" is really like the hair-drying thing, right?

Oops, mental ramble.

"Wow, great job, Seth. You're pretty cool in a crisis. You'd make a great superhero. Like Super Driving Dude. Or Super Algebra Guy. You're way better at the emergency-handling thing than I am." By the time I got to the end of my sentence, I could tell Seth felt way better.

I somehow felt way worse. A little too much boyfriend ego boosting at my own expense, perhaps?

"Anyway, what do we do now? Do you have a spare tire and a car-lifter-upper thing in the trunk?" I walked to the back of the car.

"Yeah, I have a spare tire, but I have a really bad feeling that my jack might be at home in the garage."

"Who's Jack and why is he in the garage? Can we call him? Does he have a tow truck?"

Seth looked at me and shook his head. "Sometimes I worry about you, Jess. My *jack*. The jack is the car-lifter-upper thing."

"Oh, right. Whatever. Do you have one?"

He opened the trunk. "Well, we're going to find out."

Five frustrating minutes of searching and another five of kicking the dirt on the side of the road and saying some moderately bad words later, Seth came and stood next to me where I was leaning against the side door.

"Sorry, Jess. I don't have a jack with me. We're going to have to call for help."

I held up my cell phone, so he could see the NO SERVICE display flashing in the little window. "Nope. We can't. No service. Any other ideas? I could flash into hyperspeed mode and go for help, but I hate to leave you on the side of the road, waiting."

I jumped up, suddenly freaked. "We're not near that alligator preserve again, are we? I never, ever want to see those monsters again." Before Seth and I were even dating he'd had to rescue me from an alligator. Not a pretty sight, I assure you.

"No, that's in the other direction. I don't really want to hang out here, either, but I don't see any other choice. It's not like I can lift the car up with one hand and change the tire with . . ."

We looked at each other.

I mean, *duh.* We started talking at the same time.

"I can—"

"You can—"

Seth laughed. "If you lift this corner of the car, I can change the tire."

So that was what we did. I remembered to lift with my knees like E told me, but honestly, the corner of a small car isn't all that much for somebody with superstrength to handle. I didn't even break a sweat.

Seth did, though, trying to get the tire bolt thingies off. I tried to make jokes about getting a job in a car shop, but he wasn't really talking to me. In fact, he wouldn't even look at me.

Uh-oh.

Mission accomplished, we got back in the car, and Seth moved the gearshift to D. "Jess, if you don't mind, I'd just as soon skip our picnic so I can go home and shower off the diet Coke. Is that okay with you?"

I looked at him, but he wouldn't meet my gaze. I wondered what I did wrong. (Besides dousing him with soda, I mean.)

"Sure. I smell like mashed potatoes, anyway. We can do the picnic another time."

It was only twenty minutes or so to my house, but it seemed to take a year to get there, and it was seriously quiet in the car. When Seth pulled to a stop in front of my house, he didn't even get out to open my door, like he always does. After a weird pause, I started to open my own door, then stopped.

"Seth? Are you okay?"

"Sure. Just hot and sticky. See you later."

I leaned over to kiss him good-bye, but he kind of did a subtle cheek-turning move, so my lips caught only the edge of his ear. I felt my heart sink into the bottom of my stomach and land on the ball of undigested biscuit. Whatever was wrong, it was bad.

Blinking really hard to keep from getting all teary like a girl, I climbed out of the car and rushed up my sidewalk. I didn't look back until I got to my front porch and heard the car start to drive off.

He didn't look back at all.

Jessie's Birthday Wish List

1. Something jewelryish from Seth. I really love Avielle's charm bracelet, but I don't want the same thing she got, because how lame would that be? Nothing even re-motely ringlike, because that carries way,

way too much baggage. Must think . . . must think. If he gets me another math book, he dies.

2. Lancôme's Attraction perfume. *Cosmo Girl* says guys will be totally drawn to it—and to me. Might help warm Seth up from whatever he's grumpy about.

3. DVD of *Troy*. (Hey, if Seth's gonna be mad at me, I may as well get my Orli fix!)

-4-
THIS IS NOT A DRILL

I yawned so hard I thought my face would crack wide open and leak my brains out. "I mean, really. A fire-safety assembly in high school? Isn't all that stuff so junior high?"

Lily snorted. We were sitting on the bleachers in the broiling-hot gym, waiting for some stupid firefighter-type-dude to come lecture us on the dangers of fire in a dry season. I squirmed around, trying to find a comfortable spot on the hard wooden bench.

"And shouldn't they be able to afford to get

the bleachers padded after all the bake-sale stuff we sold last month?"

Avielle elbowed me. "Shush, already. The main attraction has arrived. Ooh, boy, I think I'm joining the fire department."

We all stared, openmouthed, as five of the hunkiest guys I'd seen since moving to Skyville— heck, five of the hunkiest guys I'd seen *ever*— walked in through the side gym door.

Kelli, seated a row down and about three feet over, whistled loudly. "Oh, honey, you can do the fireman's carry on me anytime."

Ms. True, our principal, glared at Kelli from the podium. "That's enough. Settle down, kids. A few men from the Skyville FD have graciously volunteered their time to discuss fire safety with us. Please grant them the courtesy of listening quietly."

I whispered to Lily and Avielle, "For once in my life, I have to agree with Kelli." As I started laughing, I caught sight of Seth slouching against the side gym wall in jeans and a white T-shirt and looking totally hot. He was staring at me, eyes narrowed. When he caught me look-ing, he very deliberately looked from me to the firemen, then, eyebrows raised, back at me.

"If that's some kind of boy signal, I don't get it," I muttered.

"Shhh!" Lily hissed.

"All right, all right. It's just . . ." But when I turned back to look at Seth, he was gone.

Boys.

". . . safe disposal of flammable materials." The oldest guy of the bunch, who must be the fire chief or something, since he was the only one dorky enough to wear his big red fire hat indoors, was droning on about something, but nobody paid attention, because the fire dudes were demonstrating something that involved running around with a giant hose. It looked ridiculous, but they had this whole bulging-biceps thing going on that totally kept it from being boring.

Just when I got to the part in my daydream about kissing a fireman as we slid down that pole in the fire station, the fire alarm blared and snapped me out of it.

"Well, that's original. Run a fire drill during the fire-safety lecture. Could we be any more predictable?" Lily said as she grabbed her backpack and stood up.

"No kidding," I agreed, but there was something odd about Ms. True's reaction. Instead of going all principal on us, she looked worried and surprised, like she hadn't planned the fire drill at all.

I pointed this out to Lily and Avielle. "I don't

think Ms. True was expecting this. Maybe somebody pulled the alarm as a joke to get us out of this assembly."

Avielle shook her head. "I appreciate the thought, but man, oh, man, is whoever did it in big trouble if she catches him. She's not really a 'go easy on the prisoners' kind of principal."

As we stepped into the loose line made up of bored and chattering kids shuffling their way out the gym side door, I smelled it.

Smoke.

This was no drill.

(Okay, I have to admit that my first thought was to look around for a place to yank off my clothes and reveal my superhero outfit, so I could save the day. The problem, natch, is that I don't have superhero clothes. Or, as I like to say, I *so* don't wear tights and a cape. I mean, spandex is so 1980s. Euuwwwww. Not to mention that I'm not really at the whole "save the day" stage yet in my superhero training.)

Everybody else started to smell the smoke, too, and started yelling.

Kelli was louder than anybody else, of course. "It's a real fire! Help! Help! We're going to die! I'm being overcome by smoke! I think one of the firemen is going to have to carry me!" She sort of did something that looked like a swoon.

Not that I've ever seen a swoon, but from what I've read about swooning, this was definitely a fake swoon.

You know, if you say swoon five times in a row, it sounds like a made-up word. *Swoon, swoon, swoon, swoon—*

"Jessie! Earth to Jessie! We have to keep moving; you're blocking the doorway. Unless you want to get trampled like an extra in a cheesy disaster movie, get your butt in gear." Avielle shoved me, not all that gently, through the door to the sidewalk outside.

"Sorry. Brain fade for a minute. What's going on?"

But nobody answered me, because everybody was staring at the flames and smoke coming from Ms. True's office window. Luckily the fire crew was already on the job, and they'd brought their fire truck with them.

"But how bizarre is that?"

Lily turned to look at me. "How bizarre is what, Jess?"

Oops. Didn't realize I'd said that out loud.

"How bizarre is it that we'd have an actual fire on the one day that practically the entire fire department is already here?"

Avielle narrowed her eyes. "Pretty bizarre, now that you mention it. I wonder what's up with that?"

I tuned them out as they kept talking about what might have caused the fire, and channeled my superhearing to focus on the fire crew. (Sometimes this superhero stuff *rocks.* Especially when you want to get the real dirt on something.) Their voices were muffled, but I could get the gist of it.

". . . definitely set."

"We're good on the water. Got the damage . . . in time. No coincidence . . ."

". . . aisle cabinet . . ."

Aisle cabinet? Huh? No, that must have been "file cabinet."

"Arson . . . no joke. Crack down . . . kids."

Then one of the guys let loose with a string of blistering words, some of which I'd never even heard before. I shut down the channeling, quick. I prefer my supereavesdropping to be PG-rated, max.

I looked at Lily and Avielle and spoke without thinking. "They think it's arson."

"What? How do you know?" Lily tilted her head and stared at me.

"Oh. I just . . . well, the coincidence of their being here, plus they're taking an awfully long time, and . . . I don't know. It's just a guess." I could hear my voice getting grumpy, but being stupid enough to almost give away my superhearing does that to me.

Avielle looked at me like I was a space case and shook her head. "We'll ask Seth. His uncle is in the fire department, so he'll find something out tonight from his mom, no doubt."

As Ms. True called for us all to return inside to the gym, I searched for Seth in the throng huddled around the small pool of shade near the wall. When I couldn't find him, it hit me.

I hadn't seen him since that moment in the gym. Where had he gone? Had he seen the evil criminal who set the fire? Had the arsonist caught Seth watching him and hit my darling boyfriend over the head with a kerosene can, leaving him to suffer a miserable fate in the towering flames?

Or had Seth just taken a bathroom break, and I needed to quit watching so much TV?

Hmmm. I was thinking I'd go with B.

I banged the screen door open and ran inside, tossing my backpack on the couch. "Mom! Wait till you hear this. I tell you, this school is—"

I stopped dead as I heard the unbelievable, unimaginable, totally freakish sound of my mother giggling.

Giggling?

It had to be something Chloe was doing. I headed for the kitchen. "Mom, what in the world are you . . ."

But Chloe wasn't even in there. Mom was sitting on the kitchen counter, legs dangling, talking on the phone.

And, as I may have mentioned, giggling. Which is totally wrong on so many levels.

I leaned against the stove and folded my arms. "Who are you talking to, and why are you laughing like that?"

I wasn't using my "quiet voice" either, if you know what I mean.

Mom put her hand over the receiver. "Jessie, hush. I'm on the phone here. Get yourself a snack and go do your homework. I'll be up in a minute."

Leaving me standing there with my mouth hanging open, she hopped down off the counter and headed out the back door, still talking on the phone.

I snapped my mouth shut, as I figured out what had to be going on. *Oh, okay. It must be E, and they're planning my birthday party. Mom used to throw me those elaborate surprise parties before Dad died; they're probably figuring out all the details. Of course she doesn't want me to overhear. And it would be cheating to use my superhearing, no matter how much I want to. . . .*

I grabbed an apple and some fat-free crackers (which taste like wallpaper, but at least they're filling and won't make my butt any bigger) and sat down at the table to visit the exciting world of the French Revolution.

Yawn city.

I was finding it tough to concentrate and not give in to my total desire to eavesdrop at the same time, but I got all the way up to the part where some queen was giving out cake. Then Mom walked back in and put the phone on the charger. She had a smug "I know a secret" kind of expression.

"So," I asked innocently, eyelash batting and all, "who was that?"

"Nobody. It's not important." But she looked all blushy when she said it.

Mom's a terrible liar. She was totally planning my party.

"Riiiight. Okay, you go with that, Mom. *Nobody.*" I tapped my pencil on my book, right on the picture of the guillotine, although it wasn't symbolic or anything.

"No, really, Jess. I mean, it wasn't *nobody.* It was Luke. We're, ah . . . we're going out to dinner again this weekend. Can you babysit one night?" She was still pink around the tips of her ears and wouldn't look me in the eyes.

Two can play this game. I'll go along with her cover story. As if she'd be giggling like that with Sheriff Polyester.

Um, she wouldn't, would she?

Euwwww. Suddenly the crackers weighed about a hundred pounds in my stomach.

Mothers should *not* giggle. There oughta be a law.

No. It had to be about my birthday. No way my mother was acting like that over a guy she'd only gone out with for . . .

. . . about as long as I'd gone out with Seth.

No, no, no, no, no. It was totally about my birthday. End of story.

When I grabbed my books and left the kitchen, she was humming.

Jessie's To-do List

1. Help Lily keep evil Cheerleader of Death away from John.
2. Find out what's wrong with Seth (and fix it? my fault?).
3. Try to be nice to Luke. Suggest new uniform style that would use natural fibers like cotton.
4. Call E and work her for the 411 on the party.

-5-

THIS TIME IT IS A DRILL. . . .

You know you're in trouble when your orthodontist is stroking her drill like it's her pet kitten. And just when I was almost convinced to give Dr. Painful the benefit of the doubt. I hesitated at the doorway to exam room three (which they should just call torture chamber three, if truth in advertising means anything at all these days) and wondered how far I could get before she sent the tooth police after me.

I do have superspeed, after all.

Nah, Mom would be honked off. She'd dropped me off and given me a lecture on being an adult and not whining about something that was for my own good.

I tried for humor. "Um, should I leave you two alone?"

She whipped her head around and glared at me. Again with the glowy demon eyes, when I was the only one in the room. I mean, technically they weren't glowing, but she totally had the demon thing down-pat.

She even growled at me. "Get in the chair, already. I want to get you over with so I can finish calibrating my new drill. Isn't he lovely?"

I got in the chair. *He? Who* he? *What* he? I looked around for the guy—maybe a dental technician?—who was lovely.

Nobody.

"Um, Dr. Painfu—er, I mean, Dr. Payne, isn't *who* lovely?"

Or should it be "isn't *whom* lovely"? I always get those confused. One is the object form of the subject pronoun or the subject form of the pronoun's object . . . Whate*ver*.

"Who? *Who?* Are you kidding? This beautiful drill is the CRXJ-5000, the latest in dental drill technology, you . . . you . . . teenager. I have a brand-new compressor in the next room that runs all of my lovely drills. It has its very own room. My compressor room. Lovely, lovely drills." Dr. Froot Loops had practically her whole body draped over her beloved drill by this point. Not to mention that she said "teenager" like Mom says "garden slug."

This didn't add a lot to my whole happy-ortho experience.

"Look, if this is a bad time I can always reschedule my appointment," I said, climbing back out of the chair. I *so* didn't have to put up with this.

She did the freaky Jekyll-Hyde thing again, right in front of me. She closed her eyes and took a deep breath, and when she opened her eyes, Dr. Delicate Flower was back.

"I'm sorry, Jessie; did you say something?" She blinked her eyes, then beamed a huge smile at me. No hint of the crazed drill hugger anywhere.

Somehow that creeped me out even more. Kind of like "who are you and how did you hijack my orthodontist's real personality?" I shivered.

"Oh, sweetie, I'm sorry. Is it too cold in here? Let me ask my assistant to get you a warm blanket. I'll be right back." She floated out of the room, white lab coat trailing behind her. I scanned the room frantically for Ashton Kutcher, sure I was being *Punk'd*.

Nope, no Ashton. Just me and the drill, hulking menacingly beside my chair. *Great.* Now I was expecting an inanimate object to go all Professor Snape on me. I really needed to tone down the imagination overdrive.

Dr. Sweet 'n' Light came back to the room with a blanket. "All right, dear. Is that better? Now it's time to take your impressions. Most orthodontists let their assistants do this step, but I much prefer to see how the teeth fit together myself."

I hadn't wanted a blanket, but the sound of her way-too-sugary voice gave me the chills, so I wrapped it around my shoulders and watched her mix something that looked like Chloe's Play-Doh, except it was the color of old mud. Suddenly she stopped mixing and her shoulders kind of quaked. Not really a shiver—more like a shudder.

Then she whirled around and loomed over me with a plastic semicircle full of goop clutched in one hand. "Open your mouth, kid. I just loooove this part."

Oh, crap. Dr. Doom is back.

"I don't think—*Mwaghhhrrarrghh!*"

I'm suffocating she's trying to kill me this is the most disgusting glop in the world oh it tastes like raw liver not that I've ever tasted raw liver but if I had this would be just like it I can't breathe oh help help help she's coming at me

45

again what can I do what can I do she's yanking oh no she's yanking my teeth right out of my head!

"*Mwaghhhrrarrghhrrouch!* Ouch! You almost ripped my teeth out of my head! This is so disgusting! Where can I spit? Oh, yuck, oh, euuu-uwwwww, must spit." I couldn't see a bowl or a basin anywhere and was so *not* going the "rinse and suction" route. I hopped up out of the side of the chair away from Dr. Nutcase and ran for the sink in the corner, moaning and gagging.

I rinsed and spat and rinsed and spat and rinsed and spat until I had almost all of the disgustingly nasty goop out of my mouth. As I stood up and reached for a paper towel, I caught sight of myself in the small mirror hanging over the sink. I looked like a refugee from a mudslide; there were smears of brown goo all down the side of my face and on the top of my shirt, and my eyes were watering so badly that tears ran down my face.

I clenched the edge of the countertop so hard that I could feel the tile start to crumble beneath my fingers. Then I took a deep breath and turned around to face my tormentor.

She was laughing.

The evil, hideous escapee from prison dental school was laughing.

I was *so* out of there. To heck with League

policy. To heck with waiting for my mom to pick me back up. She'd just have to understand. I flashed into hyperspeed mode and was halfway down the street in about two seconds. There was no way I would ever, *ever* go back to that lunatic.

"My braces installation appointment is the day before my birthday. Plus I have to go back for a makeup appointment, since I bailed on Dr. Evil Brown Goop." I stood next to Lily in the school parking lot, waiting for Mr. Platt to bring the driver's ed car around the corner for our first lesson.

"What do you mean, you have to go back? Didn't your mom get it that your ortho is a psycho?"

Lily clearly doesn't have a mother who thinks her daughter is the queen of exaggeration, like I do: *Jessie, I understand that you don't want to have braces. Nobody wants to have braces. But you can't let a few vanity concerns get in the way of having the proper bite in the future.*

Speaking of things that bite . . .

"Is *that* the driver's ed car? No way I'm going to be seen in that." Mr. Platt was rounding the corner in a dinosaur. I mean, Mr. Platt was practically ancient, like at least forty-five or something, but this car was even older than him. An actual station wagon, wood paneling on the side and all. Did they even make that kind of car anymore?

"You've got to be kidding," I said.

"I wish I were," Lily said.

"Jessie, you're up first," Mr. Platt said.

And to think I almost liked that guy. I slid in on the plastic-covered seat carefully, trying not to let it touch any skin. Imagine how fun plastic seating is in the Florida heat, and you get a pretty good idea of my state of thrillsville. But, still, it was—if you half closed your eyes and squinted—an actual car. An actual car that I was going to be driving. How mondo cool was that?

Mr. Platt looked nervous for some reason. He kept twisting the end of his tie, and his left eye was twitching. "All right, Jessie. Let's see you put the car in drive and take a slow, sedate turn around the parking lot. I hope you're better at driving than at algebra." He laughed kind of weakly, as if even *he* realized how totally lame a thing that was to say.

I mean, how cruel is it to remind somebody of her failures just before she starts her very first driving lesson in a real car? I tried to be the bigger person and ignored him. Taking a deep breath, I carefully moved the gearshift and waited.

The windshield wipers wiped. As far as I could tell, no gears shifted.

Creak, creak, creak.

I think I hypnotized poor Mr. Platt. He just sat there for a minute, head moving back and forth to follow the windshield wipers. He didn't move a muscle, other than his head. Back and forth, back and forth.

Unfortunately, the car didn't move, either.

"Um, Mr. Platt, I think your car is so old it's defective." I hated to bring it up, knowing what school budgets were like in Florida and all, but if the gearshift didn't even work, we weren't going to get much of a lesson in.

He sighed. Hugely. "Jessie, that was the windshield wiper control, as you might have figured out by now. The gearshift is on the other side of the steering column."

Oops. He was right. There was the thingy with the P R N D D2 on it.

Uh-oh.

"Why are there two Ds? And what is 'two'? This wasn't in the book, Mr. Platt. I totally read the book. P is park, R is rearways, N is not going anywhere, and D is drive; that extra D and the two were *so* not in the book. This isn't like your pop quizzes, where you ask stuff you never told us, is it? Because I think there's a whole different level of responsibility when we're talking about thousands of pounds of potentially lethal machinery."

I stopped talking when I realized Mr. Platt was making bizarre gasping noises. *Must be the heat.* "Are you okay?"

"I . . . you . . . Jessie." He whooshed out a deep breath. "It's R for reverse. N for neutral, which disengages the engine. D for drive, and the second D is for a different gear, that we're not going to use, since we don't have any mountains in Skyville. So if you think you've lectured me sufficiently on automobile safety and my responsibilities as a teacher, perhaps we could try again?"

He sounded just the teensiest bit peeved. Maybe he hadn't taken his Geritol. You have to make extra allowances for old people.

So I tried again, and even remembered to put my foot on the brake when I moved the gear thingy to D.

Nothing happened. Again.

"Jessie, you have to take your foot off the brake and put it on the accelerator."

"Huh?"

"The gas pedal. Put your foot gently on the gas pedal." He sounded a little squeaky on that second "gas pedal," to be honest.

"Oops. Right. Move my foot and press . . . Whoa!" The car hesitated for a split second, then made a weird screeching noise and roared to life, lurching forward and slamming us back against the seat.

"Gently, *gently!* Take your foot off the gas and lightly touch the brakes. *Lightly!*"

Sheesh. Why is he getting so excited? "I'm braking, I'm braking already. I—"

Screeeeech.

"Oops. Maybe I need to work on 'gently.' " I grinned at Mr. Platt, who was clenching his teeth so hard I could see the muscles in his jaw working. It wasn't a pretty sight. He pulled a bandanna out of his front shirt pocket and wiped his forehead, which was all sweaty in spite of the air conditioner blasting on max A/C.

Then he started muttering: "I'm doomed. I'm doomed. I thought, 'Be a teacher, Harold. It's a very rewarding profession and it's safe. Can't get in a lot of trouble as a teacher.' Ha! I should have been a smoke jumper like my brother. That would have been safer than this. Easier on the nerves. Nobody even gives me a parachute. Where's my parachute?"

I could feel my eyes getting wider and wider as he kept rambling on about smoke jumping and nerve pills and disability insurance, what-ever *that* meant.

What is it about me that causes grown-ups to go wacky?

Mr. Platt closed his eyes and took a mondo deep breath, which was flashbackish to Dr. Deadly, but when he opened his eyes, it was still him. Him, Mr. Platt, I mean.

"All right. Let's try this again."

I reached for the gearshift thingy again.

"No! Ahem. Let's just talk it through before you start. First, foot on brake and shift into drive. That's D. The first D. Then, very, very gently, move your foot to the accelerator—the gas pedal—and very, very gently press down on the gas. One turn around the parking lot and we'll move on to Lily's turn."

Then he muttered something that sounded an awful lot like, "If I live that long."

-6-

HAIR STRAIGHTENERS, UNFAITHFUL GUYS, AND OTHER TRAGEDIES

After driver's ed, we waved good-bye to Mr. Platt as he stumbled off across the parking lot to his own car. He was doing the muttering thing again, causing me to have serious concerns about his mental state, but whatever. Lily and I had told the moms that we'd walk home, so we had some time to discuss the Kelli sitch.

"She cornered him today and told him that her dad is going to throw a private party for cheerleaders and the team. Just a 'football spirit thing,' as she put it. No room for dates; it's a small, *exclusive* restaurant." Lily clutched her backpack so tightly I could tell she was imagining Kelli's scrawny neck under her fingers.

"Exclusive? I'll give her exclusive. I'll ram my exclusive shoe right up her exclusive—"

"Whoa! Is this peace-loving Lily? Is this Lily of the 'I won't stoop to her level' fame?" I grinned and sneaked a look sideways at her as we walked along.

Lily kicked a stone out of her way on the sidewalk and groaned. "I know, I know. It's not at all like me, but I go all archetypal jealous woman when she pulls this crap."

"All arca-what? Stop with the big words and let's get down to business. What are you going to do about it? Because if you don't do something, before you know it she'll have John in a lip-lock and he won't even know what hit him. No offense, Lils, but he's not exactly a master strategist." I held my breath and waited for the explosion. (Even slightly negative comments about a friend's boyfriend are prohibited, unless you're actively helping her avoid a catastrophe. It's in the best-friend guidelines— right under "Never, *ever* date a guy your best friend has dated," and above "Never agree when she's calling her mom and dad hideous examples of bad parenting; just make soothing noises."

No explosion happened—Lily just sighed. "I

know, I know. He's no captain of the Chess Club. But he's so sweet and kind and funny, and you're right. He'd get sucked up in Kelli's evil plots without even realizing how it happened."

She stopped dead right there in front of Burger Haus. The smell of french fries reminded me I was starving. "Hey, you wanna get something to eat? Mom's not—"

Lily put a hand up to stop me. "Forget food. This is war. We have to have a plan."

"I plan better on a full stomach," I pointed out.

She rolled her eyes. "All right, already. Fries first, battle strategy second."

I pushed open the door to Burger Haus, smiling. "You're on."

Forty-five minutes and two extra-large fries later, we still didn't have much of a plan. We'd agreed to work as a team (we reached Avielle by cell) and block any moves Kelli made in John's direction, and Lily agreed to at least consider telling John about Kelli's plans. Then Lily took off for home, and I made one of the most life-changing decisions of my entire almost-sixteen years of existence.

I decided to stop in Meckley's Drugstore for something to calm down the frizz mop that's otherwise known as my hair.

In my defense, the box said:

Jax Abbott

PERFECTLY SAFE FOR ALL KINDS OF HAIR
EVEN COLOR-TREATED HAIR

(I can hear you groaning now. Look, it's not like *you* never tried a home perm or gave yourself a bad color job, so give me a break.)

All I could think was that maybe if Seth saw me with my new, beautifully smooth hair, he would be so overwhelmed with my total hottieness that he'd get over whatever was bugging him and getting seriously in the way of my achieving my weekly kiss quota.

So, actually, it was all Seth's fault.

"Mom! Jessie's been hogging the bathroom for an hour!"

I rolled my eyes. "Do you have to be so annoying? Is it, like, a rule or something: All little sisters must be annoying at all times? Anyway, it's only been . . ."

I glanced at the fish-shaped clock perched on the pale blue bathroom wall, blinking a little from the fumes from the hair straightener. (Yes, it had chemicals in it, but the box and even the little paper thing inside the box said, *Totally safe.)*

Oh, crap. It was already 7:20. How was it 7:20? I'd put the goop on my hair, checked the clock for when it would be ten minutes, then picked

56

up the latest issue of *Seventeen* to see what was hot in fall clothes. It had been 6:45 when I sat down on the edge of the tub, and that meant . . . fifteen plus twenty, minus the original ten . . . Oh, *serious crap,* this stuff had been on my hair twenty-five minutes longer than it was supposed to be.

I jumped in the shower, pulling clothes off like a wild woman, chanting, "Totally safe, totally safe, the box said totally safe."

I blasted the water on high and pulled the little knob to start the shower, even though it hadn't warmed up yet. "Eeeyiikes! That's cold!"

I stood there, shivering and running the water through my hair over and over, smoothing it out with my fingers.

It worked! My hair is straight! It worked! It . . .

. . . was so totally straight that it started breaking off.

In clumps.

My beautifully straight hair was snapping right off like pieces of uncooked spaghetti.

And it looked . . . odd. Straight and odd. Odd and . . . *orange?*

"My hair is orange! It's orange, and it's breaking off in the shower, and it's orange!" I shrieked, watching my broken orange hair swirl around in the bottom of the tub.

I screamed for Mom. "Mom! Help me! My hair is orange!"

I heard the door bang open and Mom's steps on the tile floor. "Jessie, I wish you'd quit exaggerating all the time. For goodness sake, if you'd just—" She pulled the shower curtain aside a little and handed a towel through to me. "Now dry off, get out here, and let me see."

I wrapped the towel around me and watched as more hair floated down to land on me, the towel, and the tub. The contrast between the white towel and my orange hair was even more gruesome. I started shrieking again.

"*Aaarghhhhhh!* How could I have been so stupid? Why does this always happen to me? My hair is ruined!"

I yanked the shower curtain back and stared at my mother.

She stared back.

For once in her life, Amy Drummond was totally speechless.

Then Chloe pushed past Mom, who'd been blocking the doorway. She took one look at me and started howling with laughter. "Jessie, you look . . . you look like Ronald McDonald, except if his hair was straight! That is the funniest color of hair I've ever seen in my whole life!"

She laughed so hard she was gasping for air and actually fell on the floor, holding her side.

"My tummy hurts. Oh, stop making me laugh so hard; my tummy hurts."

I glared at both of them through the tears that were pouring down my face. "Mom! Get her out of here before I'm the *last* thing she ever sees in her life. What am I going to do? What am I going to do?"

I took a deep breath. Maybe it wasn't as bad as I thought. I had to look in the mirror. I had to see for myself.

I stepped out of the tub and over to the mirror while Mom shooed Chloe out of the room. The mirror was fogged, but I clenched my jaw tight and wiped the steam off the glass.

It really *wasn't* as bad as I'd thought.

It was *worse*. My hair was *chrome orange!*

"Aaaaaaarrrrrrrgggggghhhhhhhhhhhhhh!"

Why was Fate punishing me like this? Was I the laughingstock of the entire universe? How could my life possibly get any worse?

Mom started to pat my shoulder, with an expression on her face like she was totally trying not to crack up.

I glared at her, then started sobbing again. "If you laugh at me, I'll . . . I'll . . ."

Rinngggg.

Oh, no. Not the doorbell.

Chloe ran for the stairs. "I'll get it."

Please, please let it be somebody selling

something. Just once, when you actually want it to be, let it be a vacuum-cleaner sales dude, or an insurance sales guy, or even space aliens. Please, please, anything but . . .

"Jessie, it's your *boyyyfriend!*"

My life is over.

I stared at Mom in openmouthed horror. "What do I *do?* I can't let him see me like this!"

Mom made a weird swallowing sound and then started grabbing bottles of shampoo and towels. "You can either cancel your date, or stall him while we try to wash some of this orange out of your hair. Hopefully it hasn't set too much. I seem to remember something about dishwashing soap being a color stripper. Although I don't understand why a hair straightener affected the *color* of your hair."

"I don't want to cancel yet. Can we try this color-stripping thing?" I was pathetically hopeful, but it was worth a shot. It *had* to work; it just *had* to.

Mom walked out to the hall and yelled for Chloe. "Chloe, make yourself useful, sweetie, and bring me some dishwashing soap right now. And I mean *now*. Seth, Jessie will be a few minutes. Please have a soda from the fridge and feel free to watch TV for a bit."

A few minutes later Chloe popped back in, clutching the bottle of dishwashing gel in her hands. "I can't wait to tell Seth about your hair, Jess. It's going to be—"

"You won't do any such thing, young lady. If you say one word about Jessie's hair to Seth, you'll be grounded from playing with Phoebe for two weeks. The Drummond women stick together in the face of catastrophe. Got it?" Mom had her "listen to me or else" face on, and Chloe backed down immediately. We knew the consequences of defying scary-faced Mom.

I felt oddly distant from the whole conversation, because the sight of my bright orange hair sticking straight out in all directions was so unbelievably hideous, it had hypnotized me.

"My life is over. I'm doomed to be a high school reject for the rest of my life."

"Calm down. Put your head in the sink and let me try to wash some of this out."

I stuck my head in the sink, praying fervently for a hair-color miracle. But thirty minutes and six washes with dish soap later, even my mother had to admit that we were defeated. "I'm sorry, honey, but this isn't doing anything. We're going to have to take you to the salon and get it stripped out. But nothing's open till tomorrow. So you'll have to cancel your date with Seth or wear a hat."

I clutched the edge of the sink and groaned. My head felt like it had been scrubbed with sandpaper after all the washings, but the orange wasn't even slightly dimmed. On the positive side, you could eat off my head, it was so clean.

I burst into tears. "I don't want anybody to eat off my head!"

Mom hugged me and patted my back. "Shhh, Jess. What in the world are you talking about? It's just a bad-hair episode. Everybody has them. Did I ever tell you about the home perm I gave myself right before my senior class pictures?"

"That's . . . that's ancient history! This is happening to me *now!* Why couldn't you give me the good-hair genes, anyway? Why didn't I get the straight blond hair like you and Chloe? This is all your fault!"

Mom stepped back a little and gave me her stern face. "Okay, enough with the self-pity. Are you going to go out with Seth, or should I send him home?"

I peered at myself in the mirror again through tear-soaked lashes. It was still orange. I snuffled a bit. Hey, I *deserved* self-pity.

"I'll wear a hat. There's nothing I can do here to fix it, and I don't want to cancel, so I'll wear a hat. Where's that old Seattle Mariners ball cap of Dad's? I can fit all my hair up under it and nobody has to know, right?"

Mom smiled at me. "That's the spirit! I'll go find the hat, and you start pinning your hair up with barrettes."

Ten minutes later I finally came downstairs in a denim mini, a blue tank with EAT AT JOE'S printed in silver along the hemline, and all of my hair tied, pinned, and stuffed under Dad's old hat. It was a look.

It wasn't a *good* look, but it was a look.

"Hey, Jess, cool hat. Ready to go?" Seth opened the door for me as I reached the bottom step. He didn't notice anything odd about my hair at all. Boys are so clueless.

I love that about them.

SuperJessie@Leagueblog.com

Hello, League-ettes and League Dudes.

What a crappy day. Yes, I had a date, but I'm home and in bed at ten, if you want to know how low I've sunk. Anyhow, if you truly want to make a difference to mankind, or at least teenagerkind, you need to invent some kind of super-hair-straightener ray gun. Or at least a hair-fixer ray gun, for when, say—and this is just a hyped-out-thetical example of some random teen superhero who never had red frizzy hair—anyway, in my totally random example, a superhero has only the very best intentions and so totally *did* read the box and the instructions, no matter what her crabby mother might think, but still managed to do mondo harm to her—or his, could be a guy, after all—hair, you could . . .

Er, what were we talking about? Let me scroll . . . Right! Hair-fixing ray guns. You need to invent them. I bet we'd make a fortune. I can, I mean, that random person could totally be in the TV infomercial.

Anyway, have you made any progress on my *not* coming to visit for my birthday? 'Cause, you know, in some cultures the sixteenth BD is, like, a sacred tradition that should never be broken for minor stuff, and plus there's gonna be cake.

Chocolate fudge cake with chocolate fudge icing.

I would be so unhappy to miss chocolate fudge cake. Especially when that's all I have to look forward to, considering my stupid boyfriend is hardly speaking to me and won't tell me why. Not that I care. Much.

Yours in super-duper-osity,

Jessie

-7-

EGGPLANT OF DOOM

"Does this dress make me look fat?"

My size-two mother stood in front of the mirror in her bathroom, turning this way and that, peering back over her shoulder at the imaginary rolls of fat she'd somehow developed in her weird parental mind.

I rolled my eyes. "No. And what happened to 'we don't say "fat" in this household and get caught up in bad body-image values that cause eating disorders'?"

Mom laughed. "Do I really sound that bad?"

"Well, you do have a lot of personal-fave

rants, but we don't have to go into that now. Tell me again why we all have to go along on your— and it makes me feel slightly gaggy to even say the word, but—*date* with Sheriff Polyester?"

Mom pointed at the doorway, and I skulked back into her bedroom and threw myself backward on the bed, being careful not to lose my grasp on my Britney Spears–like beret, which covered my very un-Britney-like orange hair.

"Plus you can tell me why, while you're at it, we couldn't get my hair fixed today. Ten thousand hair salons in the state of Florida, and you had to call the one that couldn't fit me in till Monday." I squinted at her, suspicion setting into my paranoid (and probably orange-colored; this stuff is *toxic*) brain cells.

I closed my eyes and moaned. "Is this some kind of lesson? Make Jessie have orange hair so she learns not to jump wildly into hair-chemical madness in the future?"

"Jessie, there is no lesson. No lesson, no punishment, and no conspiracy. Have we about covered all of your theories? Because I have to admit I'm getting a little tired of hearing about it. I only want to take you to somebody really good to try to get your hair repaired. Do you really want to go to a five-bucks-a-pop haircut place and let them ruin your hair even more?"

I opened one eye and peered at her, going for

the tragic face. She smiled at me and shook her head. "Orange hair. You do manage to be the least boring daughter in the history of the world; do you know that?"

I rolled over and buried my face in the soft quilt on Mom's bed. She still used the antique quilt with yellow and blue butterflies on it that she and Dad had found together at an antique shop on their honeymoon. Dad had always pretended it was too girly for him, but Mom said he'd talked her into buying it in the first place. I closed my eyes again, feeling a sting behind my eyelids.

I still miss him so much.

Mom sat down on the bed next to me and put her hand on my shoulder. "It's not a date, Jess. It's a chance for us all to get to know each other. Please give him a chance. He's a very nice man."

She stood up and walked over to the jewelry box on her dresser, then fiddled around inside. "I told you that you could bring Seth."

"Riiiight. How gross is that? Double-dating with your own mother. No, thank you." I kinda didn't mention that after last night's date—also known as the Cold Silence of Disaster—seeing Seth again didn't seem like so much fun. He hadn't said three words to me at DQ, and I was so bummed, I couldn't even bring myself to finish my triple-hot-fudge sundae. How sick is that? Then we'd walked around the mall in almost total silence, till I finally made some lame excuse to get him to bring me home.

I pushed myself up off the bed and straightened the hem of my cute new off-the-shoulder yellow tee. *To heck with him. There are other Normals in the sea. Er, in the town. Or at the mall, even.*

Yeah, right. Then why does my stomach hurt just thinking about Seth not talking to me?

I did a mental head shake and headed for the door. Enough with the self-pity. "I'll go get Chloe, Mom. Just wear the silver minihoops, already." I rolled my eyes again. (I had to quit doing that. If Mom kept dating Luke much longer, I was gonna get permanent eye sprain.)

I looked around the restaurant in surprise. It wasn't totally lame. I'd expected some kind of plastic chain restaurant, the kind that still tries to force a kids' menu and crayons on you when you're twelve. But Marcello's was the real deal—Italian food cooked by actual Italians. I could hear my stomach rumbling and hoped nobody else could.

"Jessie's tummy is growling! Jessie's tummy is growling!" Chloe grinned hugely and stuck her tongue out at me behind Mom's back.

Is it too late to find a nice family to adopt her? Somebody who lives in Antarctica, maybe?

I sighed and ignored her, being the better person and all that. Luke looked at me and smiled in a "poor you, look what you have to put up with" kind of way. I even liked him a little at that exact moment. Plus, he was kinda cute, for an old guy. Especially tonight, in his real, nonpolyester clothes.

Then he put his hand on Mom's back, and they started following the hostess to our table.

I glared at Luke's hand resting on Mom's actual person like it belonged there. Not so much with the liking, suddenly.

Luke stopped at the table behind the hostess. "Is this okay, Jess?"

Oh, right. Make with the "Include little Jessie in the decisions so she won't notice I'm groping her mother" strategy. I don't think so.

I folded my arms. "Whatever."

Mom raised one eyebrow at me, and I could tell she was trying to psychically communicate that I'd better behave or else. *Fine. I'll behave as long as Sheriff Touchy-feely keeps his hands to himself.*

As Mom took her seat next to Chloe, I smoothly maneuvered around Luke to take the seat on the other side of Mom. It's hard to make a move on somebody's mom when you have to sit across the table from her, unless you play footsie or something.

Euwwwwwwww! How nasty is that? Now I'll have to watch under the table, too.

I shoved my chair back a little, so I could divide my attention between studying his feet and keeping an eye on the rest of him. Then I practiced a kind of eye flick—up, down, up, down. Never lose sight of your target, right?

"Jessie, do you have something in your eye?" Mom leaned over and started wiping the edge of my eye with her napkin. *Great. Next she'll be spitting on her hand and wiping my face. Do mothers ever realize you're not two years old anymore?*

I jerked my head away and smiled at her around my clenched teeth. "Fine, Mother. Please keep your napkin to yourself. No parental-spit issues, either, just FYI."

Mom only laughed and leaned back and started reading the menu. She seemed awfully relaxed and happy for somebody whose back had just been assaulted by a clammy sheriff hand. I glanced at Chloe. She was chattering to Luke about what looked like a dancing olive on the kids' menu. It didn't take much to entertain Chloe; that's for sure. I had to grin. Sure, she was a pest, but she was *my* pest. Sometimes I really loved that kid.

Chloe looked up and caught me watching her.

"Hey, what's wrong, Jessie? Miss your boy-friend? No kissing for Jessie tonight! Mwah, mwah, mwah!"

Sometimes I just wanted to throttle her.

"Chloe, I swear, if you—"

"May I tell you the specials?" The yummiest voice I'd ever heard drove whatever threat I'd been about to make clear out of my head. My head turned slowly to look behind me, almost on its own, like there was some kind of mag-netic head-turning force with an Italian accent standing back there.

Hello. Oh, holy mozzarella, I'm in love. Or I would be in love, if I didn't already have a boyfriend. Although Seth was kind of mean to me last night. And here I am not two feet away from the Italian version of Orli.

"Yes. Special. You. Mmmmmm." I smiled dreamily at him, then realized he was grinning kinda funny, with his mouth quirking, like he was trying not to laugh. *Oh, crap. Was that out loud?*

Chloe didn't even *try* not to laugh. She cracked up. "Oh, Jessie's in trouble. I'm telling Se-eth you think the waiter's special. Jessie's in trouble, Jessie's in—"

She broke off suddenly, and it wasn't even be-cause of my death glare, since I couldn't raise my head to look at her. My cheeks burned, and I wanted to melt into the floor.

Luke spoke up. "Yes, we'd all love to hear the specials, as Jessie started to say. Do you have anything with chicken?"

Score one for Sheriff Polyester. I had to give him bonus points for coming to the rescue, even though it was probably part of the whole sheriff mentality. But what did that make me, the good guy or the bad guy?

Hmmmm.

". . . with a ricotta-based topping. May I start with you?"

There was a silence, and I looked up. Everyone was looking at me. I peeked out of the corner of my eye at Mr. Tall, Dark, and Hottie, and he was watching me, too, pen poised over his order pad.

Great. I totally spaced out on that. Let's continue to prove that I'm a total spazz-brain, shall we?

"Um, I'm not sure yet. Can you start with somebody else?" I mumbled, nose about an inch from my menu.

As everybody else ordered, I sank back into my funk, clutching my hat and pulling it farther down over my ears so no possible strand of orange hair could fall out. *All righty, then. My hair is totally ruined, I made like Geek Girl in front of Mr. Special, and Mom's dating life is going better than mine.*

Sign me up for the Teen Loser Hall of Fame.

"Okay, we're back to you, *signorina*. Are you ready?"

"What? Er, I mean . . . Sure. Um, I'll have the eggplant parmesan. I never order that. Thanks."

"Eggplant *parmigiana*. An excellent choice. *Grazie.*"

I shoved the menu at him blindly, afraid to look up again. Except, at the exact moment that he took the menu out of my hands, I remembered why I never ordered eggplant. *Oh, no. Oh,* no.

I never ordered eggplant because—

"Jessie, eggplant gives you *diarrhea, remember?*"

I stared in horror at my so-called mother, as her words bounced off the walls of the restaurant so loudly they probably heard them next door. Or in the next state.

Or in freaking *Italy*.

"Mom, how could you, you, you . . . We're in *public* . . . You—" As I stuttered and hissed the words at her, all I could think was, *Thank goodness the waiter is gone already.* As it was, I could never, ever, *ever* look Luke in the face again. If that total yumfest of an Italian guy had heard my mother, my life would be so totally over.

"Would the *signorina* care to order something else instead?"

Aaaaarrrrrgggghhhhhhh!

Jax Abbott

<u>SuperJessie@Leagueblog.com</u>

Hello, League persons! (Yeah, yeah, I got your e-mail about being called chicks and dudes, and I get the whole inappropriate thing. But if you want a lesson on *real* inappropriate stuff, you should walk in my shoes for a day. Except not literally. I don't really want other people's feet in my shoes—I mean, gross. Like, how do people ever go bowling? Rented *shoes?* Who invented *that* nasty concept? Euwwwwwwwwww!)

I don't even know why I'm writing this, because I have absolutely nothing superheroish to report. Except that the woman formerly known as my mother has finally gone way, way, *way* over the line. Telling the entire town about my personal internal intestines is just mondo, mondo sick and wrong. Even if the waiter hadn't been a total hottie (which he was), or if I hadn't already made a fool out of myself over the specials/special thing (which I may or may not have), and even if we didn't have to go to dinner with Sheriff Polyester (which we did, although he was kind of nice, in spite of being out to dinner with two raving lunatics and one much-tortured almost-sixteen-year-old).

In fact, we . . . oh, wait, there's a new message from you in my in-box. Hold on a sec.

To Jessie Drummond: League policy clearly states that you must present yourself for testing at League headquarters on your sixteenth birthday.

74

We sympathize with your concerns about cake, but cannot make an exception. As always, we request that you please try to contain the irrelevant chatter in your postings.

Very truly yours,

The council, League of Liberty

P.S. There was, in fact, some support for a committee to look into the hair-straightening ray gun issue.

Blog, part two: Oh, sure irrelevant chatter. Very nice, when you admit there *are* possibilities in the hair-straightening market. Whatever. This conversation is *so* not over.

Yours in superstubbornness,

Jessie

IM from Lives4Art@skyvillenet.com
Hey, where have U been? How went the big getting-to-know U dinner? Is he nice? Was it fun? Lily.

SuperJessie@skyvillenet.com says:
Oh, yeah. It was great fun in the "most hideously embarrassing night of my life" sense of fun. My so-called mother—and I'm totally sure I'm adopted—told the entire restaurant, including the hottest guy I've seen outside of a movie theater, that eggplant gives me diarrhea. *Aarghhhh!*

IM from Lives4Art@skyvillenet.com
Really? That bites massively! It must be something in the properties of the plant. Is eggplant a fruit or a vegetable? I should Google it and

SuperJessie@skyvillenet.com says:
Hellooooo? So missing the point, Lils. 2 embarrassed 2 live here, and U R babbling about eggplant. <massive eye rolling>

IM from Lives4Art@skyvillenet.com
Sorry, sorry. U R right. But U shouldn't be noticing other hotties when you have a boyfriend, anyway, right? ☺

SuperJessie@skyvillenet.com says:
What boyfriend? He never even called me today, after he gave me the cold elbow all last night on our pathetic excuse for a date. And he didn't even notice that I had orange hair. Am I suddenly fading into the woodworm?

IM from Lives4Art@skyvillenet.com
Um, that's cold *shoulder* and wood*work,* Jess. Unless they have really, really different clichés and old sayings in Seattle . . . LOL! Wait—you have *orange hair?!*

SuperJessie@skyvillenet.com says:
Long story about the hair. Tell you later.
And *whatever*. Elbow, shoulder, who cares?
There wasn't any lip action, if we're gonna
talk body parts. <sigh> I think

IM from PythagorusRules@skyvillenet.com:
Hey, Jessie. Are you online? This is Seth.
*Duh. Like I don't know his screen name
by now.*

SuperJessie@skyvillenet.com says:
Yeah, I'm here, what's up?

SuperJessie@skyvillenet.com says:
Lily, it's Seth. I have to see what he wants.
BRB.

IM from Lives4Art@skyvillenet.com
OK, gotta go call John. TTYL. Be nice!

SuperJessie@skyvillenet.com says:
I will if *he* will.

IM from PythagorusRules@skyvillenet.com:
You will if who will what? Who's "he"?
Oh, crap. I've gotta quit doing that.

SuperJessie@skyvillenet.com says:
Nothing. Must have been spam or something. Although don't you wonder why they call useless mail the same name as cans of processed meat food? Totally nasty, if you think about it. Like how they

IM from PythagorusRules@skyvillenet.com:
Jessie? Not that the Spam discussion isn't interesting, but can we talk for a minute? About something else?
Let me guess. Seth thinks I'm irrelevant, too. He's really the one who should be in the League of Liberty. He has a board stuck far enough up his . . . Pythagorean Theorem.
Ha! Math humor. Who says I'm not intellectual?

IM from PythagorusRules@skyvillenet.com:
Jess? Are you there?

SuperJessie@skyvillenet.com says:
I'm here. What do you want to talk about? And why now? You didn't have much to say last night, for example.

IM from PythagorusRules@skyvillenet.com:
I know, and I guess I just wanted to say I'm sorry. The whole tire-lifting thing

weirded me out, you know? I mean, we were stuck and you just . . . well, you know what you did. And I did nothing. A guy's supposed to be able to take care of things, or at least be stronger than his girlfriend. It's bad enough you think I'm a math geek, already. I hate the idea that

IM from PythagorusRules@skyvillenet.com:
Stupid IM cut off. I hate the idea that you think I'm a wimp.

SuperJessie@skyvillenet.com says:
Seth, it's so sweet and sensitive that you would think that about wanting to take care of things, but it's also totally dumb. I mean, isn't this, like, the twenty-first century already? Not to get on Mom's wagon train, but women can take care of themselves these days. Plus, there's the whole . . . you know . . . thing.

IM from PythagorusRules@skyvillenet.com:
The thing? *What* thing? And trust me, I know all about the twenty-first century woman. My mom's a patent lawyer, for Pete's sake. But it's hard on a guy's ego when his girlfriend has to lift the car. Okay? That's all. I know it's stupid, and I'm trying

to get over it. It's my thing, not yours. And what thing?

SuperJessie@skyvillenet.com says:
Well, since you mentioned it, the SH thing. You know, the car-lifting thing? We're not really supposed to talk about it on an unsecure e-mail communication, in case some bad guys are hacking me or something. No biggie.

IM from PythagorusRules@skyvillenet.com:
<Smacking forehead> Great. Now I probably got you in trouble. I'm stupid, *and* I'm experiencing some kind of throwback to my inner-caveman mentality all at once. Sorry, Jess. Gotta go shave my back or club a dinosaur or something. Stupid, stupid, stupid. Seth.

SuperJessie@skyvillenet.com says:
Seth, no—it's no big deal! I'm sorry I even mentioned it! It was totally cool that you were strong enough to tell me about your issues with the SH thing, and I

SUBSCRIBER   PythagorusRules@skyvillenet. com IS NOT AVAILABLE.

Aaarghhhhhh! How could he hang up on me like that? Boys! Buzzzzzzzzz!

Huh? Now I'm buzzing with despair? This is new.

Buzzzzzzzz!

Oh. Right. E.

I jumped out of the computer chair and looked around for E's buzzy box. She'd given it to me before she went back to her island; it was kind of a cross between a pager and a cell phone and it could detect my presence from my vibes or something. So I could basically never "let the machine answer."

"Jessica Drummond? I know you're there! Answer right this instant." E's voice sounded tinny, but muffled, and I finally found the ring-sized black box under a pillow on my bed.

I moved the pillow aside and watched Buzzy unfold itself like a weird, electronic black spider. If boxes were spider shaped. Or had panels instead of legs. Or . . . whatever.

"Yes, E? What's up? Did you call because you've already heard clear down there in the Bermuda Triangle that eggplant gives me diarrhea? Or that my perfectly wonderful boyfriend has suddenly developed inferiority issues because I lifted his car? So maybe he can just dump me now and find some lame girlfriend who couldn't even help fix a flat tire?"

I switched to a squeaky, high-pitched whine: " 'Oh, no, Sethie, I can't help you! I might break one of my stupid Normal fingernails on my stupid Normal hands, but at least you won't have to be freaked out because I'm stronger than you are.' "

I stopped to heave in a breath. "Wench! I hate her already! And what is she doing in my boyfriend's car with him in the first place? Does she think he'll get over me so easily? He'll be pining away for me for, like, months! Or years. Yeah, years, even. Ha! That'll show her! I'll—"

"Jessie? Dear? Light of my life? What the *heck* are you talking about?? Are you actually plotting the downfall of Seth's imaginary girlfriend?"

I closed my mouth midbreath and thought about it.

Yeah, pretty much. Way over my psycho nutjob quota for the month here. Please fit me for my straitjacket.

"Never mind, E. What's up?"

"Well, other than your adrenaline level, obviously, what's *up* is your birthday trip to the League. I'm coming to practice for the trials with you. Be there tomorrow."

"Wait! Trials? What trials? I thought it was just a schmooze thing, 'Hey, I'm Jessie, how ya doin'?' kind of deal. What's this about trials?"

"I'll be there tomorrow and tell you every-thing. Don't worry about it. Get some sleep. 'Bye."

Click.

I stared blankly at the tiny black box as it furled back up, walls closing in on it. Kind of like my life.

Right. Don't worry. Let's see. . . .

1. My boyfriend thinks dating me makes him a wimp.
2. My mother hates me after I bailed on her special dinner, and wouldn't even speak to me when she got home a couple of hours after I hypersped out of there.
3. The entire universe probably knows by now that I have Eggplant of Doom issues.
4. There are trials. At the League of Liberty.

Seriously, why would I worry?

-8-

TESTING, TESTING . . .

Say what you want, E is all about making an entrance. She banged the door open, took one look at me, and bellowed, "*What* did you *do* to your *hair?*"

I glared at my grandmother as she walked in the door, then realized there was a much better comeback than making faces at her.

I smiled my most sickeningly sweet smile. "Why, hello, *Grandmother*. Did you have a nice flight, *Grandmother?* Would you like to rest your tired *grandmotherly* bones after your journey?" E *despises* being called Grandma or, much worse, *Grandmother.* She thinks it makes her sound old. Which is a riot, since she doesn't look any older than Mom, but in a tall, red-haired, black-leather-boots, gorgeous kind of way.

"May I get your bag for you, *Grandmother?* I wouldn't want you to wear yourself out." I hopped out of the chair, still grinning.

E burst out laughing. "Okay, okay, I get it already. I should have said 'hello' and 'nice to see you' before I mentioned the hideous orange. So, hello! Nice to see you. How are you? What did you *do* to your hair?"

I sighed. She'd never change.

Thank goodness.

"It's a looong story, E. Got a week or two?"

"Focus, Jessie. Focus!" E sounded disgusted with me, which was totally unfair, since I was really trying. I just kept getting distracted.

Plus, I really, *really* needed to scratch my leg. The one I was standing on, not the one held out at a forty-five-degree angle. The teensy problem was that my hands were full with the massively heavy wooden picnic table from our backyard.

The one I'd been holding over my head for twenty minutes.

While E, Chloe, and Mom sat on it, drinking lemonade and chatting.

It itches, it itches, it itches!

"I have to scratch my leg or I'm gonna die," I said. (Well, okay, I whined, but the sitch totally deserved a little whining.)

"Nobody dies from a little itchiness, Jessica. Change legs."

I never wanted a grandmother, anyway. We were doing just fine without the evil tyrant. We just minded our own business—

"Now!"

"All right, all right already." I slowly lowered my left leg to the ground and breathed a sigh of relief at the sensation of having both of my feet supporting me at the same time. I was superstrong, but I never exactly worked out, and the stand-in-one-place-on-one-leg thing was killing me.

"Jessica, lift the right leg now. Ten more minutes; then we'll have dinner."

"Fine." I knew I sounded surly, but again with the *so* deserved. I started to lift my right leg (and I'm right-handed, which I think makes me right-legged, too; or at least I know I felt a whole lot steadier when I was standing on my right leg.)

I felt like I was getting steadier; then I heard a noise outside the fence. *What if it's Seth? What if he sees me holding up my entire family on this table, after our whole "don't really want a girlfriend who's stronger than me" talk?*

I listened really, really hard, but didn't hear any more sounds from the fence area. I even switched on the superhearing. Nothing.

The evil snark in my head wouldn't give up, though. *What if it* is *Seth, and he saw us through the fence, and now he's super, super mad at me and is leaving and will never come back?*

Um, duh. You do *have X-ray vision, moron,* I said to myself.

Oh, yeah, I replied to myself.

I squinted my eyes at the fence and, right on cue, the boards did that shimmery thing and then vanished. It looked like a jaggedy-edged hole had been burned right in the middle of the fence, and there—right in the middle of the space—I could see my neighbor's dog sitting in our lawn and scratching himself. No Seth anywhere. *Stupid dog. Well, I mean, he is kind of a cute dog, but enough is enough. Doesn't he know I'm trying to focus here? And if I have to—*

Shriiieeeeeekkkkkkk!

My head slammed back on my neck from the force of the hideous noise crashing through my ears. I blinked, and my X-ray vision went kerplooey. Just *wham,* and the entire fence was there again, blocking my view of Spot.

The noise continued until I thought my teeth would surely explode. *Ha! That would show Dr. Psycho. Can't get braces if you don't have teeth.*

The decibel level of the shrieking jolted upward. The pain in my ears rocketed through my skull. "Mom! E! What *is* that? Help me!"

I couldn't hold on to the table and deal with the noise all at once. I could hear Mom and E chatting and laughing with Chloe, like they hadn't even heard me. My hands got sweaty. I could feel the table slipping out of my grasp. I started to wobble a little.

Then I started to wobble a *lot.*

"I don't think I can do this with my left leg. . . . I'm having trouble . . . I'm . . . Oh, crap. *Help!*" My leg wobbled so hard it wouldn't hold me up. I slammed my right foot back down on the ground, but it was too late; the wobbling had spread.

I couldn't stop. . . . *"Help!"*

My knees both went hinky at the same moment. I crashed down to the ground with only a split second to anticipate the weight of the enormondo table on its way to crush me into an ugly smear of splattered superhero.

I clenched my eyes shut. (No sense facing death by picnic table with your eyes open.)

All I could think was, *I'm gonna die, I'm gonna die, I'm gonna die. . . .*

Why didn't I die?

I opened one eye and looked around.

Nope, not dead.

I opened the other eye and looked up.

The picnic table floated over my head, and Mom, Chloe, and E were peering down at me over the edge. Mom had her worried face on, but E had that clenchy-teeth thing happening that meant she was ticked off.

"Jessie, are you all right, honey?" said Mom.

"That was wimpy, Jess," said Chloe.

"Jessica, that was terrible," said E.

"Thanks for your concern," said Jessie. (Er, I mean, said me. Or said I. What*ever.*)

I rolled over and out from under the table, so Mom could levitate it back down to the ground. Then I stood up and brushed dirt and grass off of my new white capris. (Note to self: Never wear white after Labor Day, especially if doing hideously dangerous superhero testing.)

Mom gently floated the table to a resting spot in the yard and jumped off and rushed over to me. "Honey? Are you okay?"

I let her hug me for a second, then moved back a little. Tough superheroes didn't need to get hugs from their mommies, even if the mommy in question was finally talking to her daughter again after the dinner-with-Luke disaster.

Chloe wandered over and hugged me briefly,

then announced that she needed a cookie and wandered off. I turned my head a little to watch her go and flinched as a freight train of a headache roared through my skull. "What was that horrible noise, Mom? It hit me right in the superhearing so hard, I thought my brain was gonna melt. Where did it come from?" I rubbed my head as I talked, not so sure even now that my brain was free of the melting worry.

She looked at me kinda funny. "What noise, Jess?"

"That brain-melting metallic buzzy noise. How could you not hear it? It was like finger-nails on a chalkboard. Well, maybe if a hundred robots scraped their roboty fingernails down an electric chalkboard. All at the same time. Really, really loudly." I shuddered and clutched my head.

Seriously, there should be a higher grade of pain reliever for superheroes. Regular, extra-strength, and superhero strength. I should suggest that. . . .

"She didn't hear it. Only you and I did. It's tuned to a special frequency that ordinary hu-mans—and even most superheroes—can't hear." said E, as she stepped off the table in that elegant way she had of doing stuff.

Mom and I both looked at her.

"What did you do, Mom?" said my mom to her mom. (Hel*lo,* can you say, "too many moms in the yard"?)

And *my* mom didn't sound happy.

"It's going to be part of the test, Amy. The League council will require her to demonstrate control over more than one of her powers at the same time." E pulled something out of her pocket that looked like her little buzzy communicator box, and flicked her nail over a teensy dial.

"Ouch!" I clutched my head again, covering my ears as the horrible noise screeched out of the box at me. I notice that E flinched just a bit, too, but if I hadn't been watching really close, I never would have seen it. Amazing how she kept her face perfectly composed with that horrible thing squawking less than three feet from her head.

I was totally cool and composed, too. Except for the part where I wanted to throw up.

"Shut it down, shut it down. *Shutitdownnow!*"

"E! Shut it off!" Mom was yelling now. It was cool that she stuck up for me, but I could've lived without the extra noise, to be honest.

E flicked the switch again, and the shrieking stopped instantly. I kinda collapsed on the ground, clutching my head and moaning. *My poor ears.*

I unclenched my eyes and took a deep breath, then whooshed it out and slowly took my hands off my ears. *Okay, maybe I'm not dying.* I looked up at Mom and E as they stood there watching me, and I started to open my mouth to tell them I was okay.

E beat me to it. "She's dead."

It looked like the Magic Kingdom had exploded in my living room.

"Um, Mom? Are you kidding? You want to use Disney princess decorations for my sixteenth birthday? Please tell me that this is a bad joke." I could feel my lip curling, but couldn't make it stop.

. Mom looked up at me from where she sat on the floor, surrounded by an explosion of mermaids, glass slippers, and Prince Charmings. (The party favor, plate, and napkin kind—not the actual prince, sadly. Although Prince Charming always seemed a little girly to me, kind of like the one in *Shrek 2*, who was just gross.)

"I'm sorting through our party supplies bin to see what we need to get for your birthday Saturday. We have so much of this left over, I was just thinking maybe we could do a kind of retro party, with all the girly stuff. It might be fun, and—"

I looked at her like she was nuts. "Are you

nuts? I'm already the loser laughingstock of the tenth grade. Why don't we just tattoo a giant L on my forehead now and get it over with?"

Mom sighed and looked back down at the floor, then took a deep breath. "Jessie, what's up with you? I keep trying to make excuses for you because you're going through so much now, but can't we have one single pleasant conversation?"

"Mom, that's not fair, and you know it. You're the one who publicly humiliated me— like I need anybody's help!—at the restaurant. You're the one who's only excited when Luke's around. You're the one who cared more about which earrings to wear on your date than about the fact that my hair is totally ruined forever, and *I have to go to school like this tomorrow!*"

I paced back and forth in front of the couch. "On top of that, now you want to give me the kind of party decorations that Chloe would want at *her* party, and make me a social outcast. Do you even see me anymore, Mom? Do you even remember who I am?"

I realized the tears that had been waiting for their chance since the disaster with the picnic table earlier had escaped and were streaming down my face, and I scrubbed them away. "Did you even hear what E said? That I'm dead?

Dead? What the heck is that supposed to mean? Are they going to kill me if I fail? Do you even care? Nobody talked about it—it was all, 'Jessie, get cleaned up for dinner.' "

I took a huge breath and stopped pacing. "Dinner? Like I care about meat loaf when my life may be in jeopardy? And not only am I dying, but I'm getting leftover pink party favors? Is there no *end* to my tragedy?"

Mom jumped up from the floor and tried to hug me, but I kinda backed away. *So* not in the mood for hugging right then. Plus, I hated crying in front of anyone.

Ever.

"Honey, you're not dead. You know E is prone to exaggeration. She just meant that we need to work on your focus before the test. Please don't worry about it."

She picked up a gold-foil-covered crown. "And I don't see what's so bad about this. If we—"

I grabbed the stupid paper crown out of her hand and sent it sailing across the room. (Factor in the superstrength, and that crown flew for a long, long time. *Wow!*) Mom and I both watched it in silence, as if hypnotized. When it smashed against the window, it broke the spell for both of us. We both started to talk at the same time.

"If you think—"

"I'm not—"

". . . too old to have a pink party with my mommy!" I spat out. It's not like she cared about putting on a party for me, anyway. She'd probably rather talk to her precious Luke. It was amazing how much that thought hurt me, kinda like a hot poker in my stomach.

". . . you—*What?* A party with your mommy?" The look in Mom's eyes as she repeated my words made me realize that I wasn't the only one in the room hurting.

"Mom, I'm sorry. I didn't mean that. It's just that—"

But she wasn't listening. She was already on her way up the stairs. Halfway up, she turned to look at me, and I was sure I saw traces of dampness on her cheeks. "No worries, Jess. The last thing I'd inflict upon you is a party with your *mommy.* The party is off. You can spend your birthday with all of your oh-so-grown-up friends."

She turned and almost ran up the rest of the stairs.

"But Mom, I'm sorry. Please . . ." But Mom didn't have superhearing. She didn't even hear my lame attempt at an apology.

Suddenly I was the only one in the room.

Jax Abbott

SuperJessie@Leagueblog.com

Dear Council Members,

In the (very unlikely, really, almost no way it will happen—let's just say practically impossible) event that I couldn't quite pass my trials on Saturday (which *is* my birthday, remember, so I should get some special kind of birthday pass, don't you think?), how long would it be until I could try again?

Not that this is a problem or anything, because it's not, but I'm kind of tired this week, and I have to get braces Friday, and the pain of getting them on is supposed to be hideous, and what if the metal on the edges pokes into my gums and makes me bleed, which would be totally distracting? Would that be metabolizing circumstances? I mean, would I get a break?

Also, do you have any quaint old sayings, like "Being a superhero means never having to say you're sorry"?

TTYL,

Jessie

WHEN HAVING ORANGE HAIR IS THE LEAST OF YOUR PROBLEMS, YOU KNOW YOU'RE IN TROUBLE OR: MY HIDEOUS DAY, IN BITE-SIZED PIECES

Really, is there any problem in life that can't be cured by sitting through algebra class? *Aarghhh.* I stared at my desk, which was pretty much all I could see, since I was slouched so low in my chair that I couldn't even see over Kelli's shoulders. (And how lucky is that, to get to sit behind Kelli and her bucket o' perfume all year? *Not.*)

I raised my head suspiciously, clutching my hat with both hands, when the sound of paper shuffling broke into my gloom. Mr. Platt somehow appeared right in front of me with a stack of paper.

I hate when they sneak up on you.

He handed me a quiz and moved on down the aisle. "Pop quiz, class. You've had all weekend to brush up on these problems; this should be a snap for you."

"Right. Like we spent the weekend doing algebra," I muttered.

"What was that, Jessie?" Mr. Platt's tone didn't sound all that happy. *Crap. Maybe I could add detention to my lovely day.*

"Nothing, Mr. Platt. Just said what a great weekend it was to do algebra." I rolled my eyes and caught sight of Lily fighting to hold in a laugh.

"Yes, it was, wasn't it? Although there's never a bad time for algebra," Mr. Platt said, kind of humming.

Never a bad time for algebra. I should get a T-shirt made.

I heroically resisted the urge to bury my head in my arms on my desk and moan loudly. Then I looked at the quiz.

I buried my head in my arms on my desk and moaned loudly, careful not to dislodge my hat. All I needed was for Kelli and her gang to catch sight of my orange hair. I'd have to go into the Witless Protection Program.

"Jessie!" Lily hissed. "Stop it! What's wrong with you today? Do you want to end up stuck in Ms. True's office when we have . . . work to do?"

"No. Sorry. Nothing," I mumbled, feeling my cheeks get hot. Great, now even my best friend was ticked off at me. And I only had—I glanced at my watch—fifteen minutes to do ten of the hardest algebra problems in the history of the universe.

Piece of cake.

"I hate cake." I kicked a stray pencil down the hall, remembering at the last minute to curb my superstrength so the pencil didn't wind up embedded in somebody's locker. Or, worse, somebody's leg.

"What? What are you talking about, cake?" Lily slowed her long-legged stride to match my stubby-legged one.

"Nothing. I'm just sure I failed that quiz. I hate being a math moron." I bit my lip and tried to shake it off. No sense carrying my quiz-bomb-itis mood around with me all day.

"Why don't you get darling Sethie to help you?" Lily grinned, not realizing that my love life was currently not the brightest part of my world.

Although, come to think of it, what *was* the brightest part? *Any* bright spot? A glimmer? A teensy speck of candlelight, even?

I sighed.

"Seth and I are kind of . . . weird at the moment," I admitted.

"Why? Commitment phobia? Is he having some kind of adverse reaction to having a serious girlfriend?" Lily nodded knowingly, always happy to have somebody *else's* life to analyze.

Okay, that wasn't fair, but I'm not really in a fair mood.

"No, it's nothing. No adverphobia. Just a minor glitch. You're right. I'll ask him." I stopped in front of the door to English class and took another deep breath. *Why does every moment feel like another opportunity for disaster?*

"Jessie, you have to take the hat off in class. It's the dress code; no hats in class."

The evil villain formerly known as Mr. Sherman, my English teacher, smiled at me pleasantly.

He has some nerve.

"No! I mean, I can't. I mean, I have total hathead now. No way I can go through the rest of the day like this." I knew I was babbling, but the horror crashed over me in waves, leaving me fumbling for words.

"I'm sorry, Jessie, but rules are rules. You can go to the ladies' room to brush your hair, but I expect you back in five minutes." He stood there, arms folded, like the Grim Reaper of Orange-haired Doom, waiting for me to get out of my seat and head for the door.

I slowly stood up, aware of every eye in the room on me. (Trust me, it's as terrible as it sounds.) I grabbed my backpack, as if I had some magic brush inside that would make my hair *not* orange, and then slunk toward the door.

On my way down the aisle, Mike made a kinda fake grab for my hat, as if he wanted to yank it off. I ducked to the side, skewering him with my worst death glare. He just grinned with that unconcerned football-quarterback grin.

And to think I'd actually once wanted to kiss that loser. *Gross.*

I glanced at Seth out of the corner of my eye. He had his head down, staring at his notebook, and wasn't looking at me at all.

I almost made it. Almost.

But then I ducked my head to stare at the ground and didn't even see Kelli reach out her bony arm toward my head till the last minute. Then it was like a slo-mo instant replay. I started to yell slooooooowly, "Noooooo," and saw the hand of destruction reaching for my head, for my hat, for my hideous orange-haired head.

"Nooooo!"

But it was too late.

I stood there, frozen in horror, as Kelli yanked the cap off my head. The room erupted in laughter, a gruesome, shocking, repulsive wave of evil laughter.

They laughed at me. They laughed at my hair. As I stood, feet unable to move, I looked at Mr. Sherman. I could tell he was fighting not to laugh. That snapped me out of my paralysis and I made a break for it, feeling the sobs trying to volcano their way out of my throat. Once I made it to the hallway, I headed straight for the bathroom, desperately trying not to cry. You know, there were days when being a boy didn't seem so bad. Boys didn't. . . .

Boys didn't. . . .

Bingo. School-nurse time.

"How'd you escape? I thought you were going to have to suffer the orange-hair stigma for the rest of your life. But then you just never came back. Here's your notebook, by the way." Lily was waiting at the school front door when I rushed down the hall at lunchtime.

I jerked my head around to make sure nobody'd heard her. "Shh! Do you want everybody to know?"

Lily looked at me and shook her head sadly. "Jess, Kelli is going to have this story spread around the whole school before lunch is over. You're dead."

I whooshed out a breath. "You know, I'm awfully tired of hearing the D-word lately."

As we walked out the door into the killer Florida noontime sun, I squinted around for Mom. She was letting me get out of school early for emergency hair repair, which put her back up in the top-ten-moms category to me. I just hoped she was talking to me again.

Lily poked me in the arm. "Well? Did you just cut class? Not that anyone would blame you."

"Of course not. I'm not a total moron! I went to see the nurse and said I had killer cramps. She gave me some pain relievers and let me rest there for a while. I *love* being a girl." I grinned a little, remembering my escape, cheered up in spite of my impending doom.

"Do you?" Lily asked.

"Do I what?" I asked.

"Do you have cramps?"

We stopped at the sidewalk, and I did one of those "duh!" faces at Lily. "No, I don't have cramps. What I *have* is orange hair. But that doesn't get you a 'get out of class free' pass."

I saw the enormondously fab sight of Mom's car pulling up to the curb. "Gotta run, Lils. Say good-bye to Fright Wig Jessie! I am so totally gonna get this hair disaster fixed now."

* * *

"There's no way I can fix this hair." Gail looked at my hair with a rather greenish "I'm gonna yark" expression plastered on her face. (This was Gail the Wonder Beautician, in case you're wondering. The one I'd waited all weekend with a headful of *orange hair* to see.)

"What did you *do* to it?" She circled around me, step by step, and kept reaching out as if to touch my hair, then yanking her hand back.

I folded my arms across my chest and huddled in the chair. "It's not *contagious.*"

Mom stopped me mid-eye-roll with one of her looks. "Gail, is there anything you can do for Jess? Some kind of deep conditioning and color fixer, maybe? Trim the hair that's breaking off?"

Gail looked from me to Mom and back at me, shaking her head. "I don't know, Amy. This is the worst I've ever seen."

Suddenly she clutched her throat dramatically. "Jessie, you didn't . . . you didn't use . . . *bleach* on your hair, did you?"

"No, I'm not an idiot. The box said 'safe.' " I leaned over to dig the stupid, lying box out of my backpack and shoved it at Gail. "See? '*Safe* for all hair, even color-treated hair.' Mine's not even color-treated, so I thought I'd be fine. I'm gonna sue!"

Gail pulled her glasses off her head and put

them on and started reading. "You only left it on for the required amount of time, right?"

"Um, well. That's, um . . . well." I squirmed in the chair a little, looking anywhere but at Gail and Mom.

They both stared at me. (Mom hadn't heard this part of the story before.)

"Um, would it affect what you're going to do with my hair if I'd left the goop on just a teensy bit longer than the box said?"

Mom put her hands on her hips and groaned, and Gail made a little moaning noise.

Gail recovered first. "How much longer?"

"Um, twenty-five minutes longer?" I scanned the ceiling and grinned a big, toothy, "twenty-five extra minutes isn't really a problem, is it?" grin.

Gail shrieked and dropped the box. "Twenty-five . . . *Twenty-five minutes longer?* Are you out of your mind?"

"Um, is that a rhetorical question? 'Cause I learned about those at school, which seems to mean that you don't really want the answer, but, speaking of answers, actually I just want to know: Can you fix it?" (I was a little loud on that last part.)

Gail walked around me one last time, then seemed to come to a decision.

"How do you feel about a crew cut?"

* * *

Three hours, four deep-conditioning treatments, five minutes' worth of a color rinse, and six chewed-off fingernails later, I looked in the mirror and started to cry.

"You fixed it! Gail, you're a miracle worker! I look just like me again, only even better! And this haircut rocks!" I jumped out of the chair and threw my arms around my wonderful, awesome hairstylist.

"Thank you, thank you, thank you!" I let go of her quick when she flinched. *Ix-nay on the ooperstrength-say.* Then I grabbed the mirror to look at the back of my head again. Gail had done the top-secret super-whammodyne hairdrying trick that leaves even the bushiest hair silky and shiny. I loved it, loved it, loved it. She'd cut a few inches off the length, so my hair swung gently around the tops of my shoulders, plus done something layery to make it float around instead of looking like an actual bush on my head. The color was almost exactly what it had been *pre*–hair tragedy, but a teensy bit brighter. Brighter I could live with—orange, not so much!

I had to go scope out Seth, so I could *accidentally* run into him.

Mom had taken off two hours before to pick Chloe up and fix dinner, so I was on my own to get home. Luckily, the salon was pretty close to my house. Seth's house was on the way to mine, too, so it worked out perfectly. (Well, in a "go three blocks north, then six blocks east" kind of on the way.)

Gail started sweeping up pieces of orange hair from the floor, probably before any of her other clients saw it and thought it was her fault. She paused and grinned at me. "I'm so glad we could fix it, Jess. Now what did we learn?"

I clasped my hands behind my back and parroted back the phrase she'd been drumming into my head for three solid hours. "I will never, ever, ever touch my hair with any chemical harsher than shampoo."

"Perfect! Your mom took care of the bill. Why don't you head home and show her our miracle?"

I danced around in a circle, peering back over my left and then right shoulder at my totally unorange reflection. "Okay. I will. And thanks! Thank you, thank you, thank you!"

Gail laughed. "You're welcome. Now get going."

So I brushed a few stray strands of fright-wig hair off my pants and floated to the door. I waved good-bye to Gail as I opened the door and then turned, humming, to face my bright and shiny orange-free future.

That was when I walked right into Seth hugging another girl.

So you miss a lot of e-mail when you're getting your hair fixed and your heart broken.

DramaQueen@skyvillenet.com says:
Hey, I've been trying to IM you all evening, Jessie. We need a strategy session. When I was in the hardware store after school, buying paint for Drama Club, guess who I saw?
Mike. And guess what he was doing?
Buying paint thinner. Which Lily says is *highly flammable*. As in, catches stuff on fire. I heard him tell Mr. Romano that he needed it for Drama Club, 'cause he was painting sets and all. Mr. Romano went on and on about "What a great young man, football and drama club, blah blah blah."
But guess what again? Mike isn't *in* Drama Club. He doesn't have anything to *do* with Drama Club. So why would he lie? And what is he doing with flammable stuff? Avielle.

Lives4art@skyvillenet.com says:
Where R U? Kelli was hanging all over John at football practice. Can I kill her?

Can I? Please? Lily, contemplating cheer-
leadercide.

To Jessie Drummond: In the event—unlikely
or not—that you do not pass your trials on
Saturday, you will be removed from your
home and fostered with a council member
for the duration of your training, for a time
period to be no longer than five years.
  Have a nice day.
  Very truly yours,
  The Council, League of Liberty

-10-

KISSES AND CREAMED BEEF

I dawdled as long as I could at home, and even played find-the-green-clovers-in-the-cereal with Chloe, but still managed to make it to school about ten minutes before the bell. Since the last thing I wanted to do was run into Seth, I lurked by the girls' bathroom for a while, figuring that was totally the last place he'd ever want to be seen.

"Oh. Hi, Seth." (I'm seriously bad at hiding from people.)

I looked down at the floor, then remembered

110

that *he* was the one cheating on *me*. I wasn't the one who should be hanging my head.

"What do you want? Shouldn't you be hanging out with your new girlfriend?" I sneaked a quick look around to make sure the coast was clear. "Your new *Normal* girlfriend?"

Seth dropped his backpack on the floor and put his hands on my shoulders. "Jessie, I was afraid of this. When you disappeared—and I mean literally disappeared; you should be careful of using hyperspeed in public like that—I figured you got the wrong idea. That was just the girl—"

"Who you were dancing with at Mini Prom," I muttered, remembering very clearly the girl who'd tried her best to snag Seth for her boring Chess Club self.

"Right. Well, anyway. She just found out her parents are getting divorced, and she wanted to talk to somebody. That hug you saw was just kind of a 'sorry you're having a rough time' hug."

He grinned, and his yummy golden-brown eyes sparkled (which is *so* unfair, if you ask me). "There's only one person I want to hug in a 'I'd really like to be kissing you this very minute' way."

Then, as if I hadn't already melted into a big,

gooey puddle of warm superhero, he pulled me around to the other side of the water fountain, behind the edge of a wall of lockers, and did just that.

The hug thing. The kiss thing, too, actually. It was . . . *Mmmmmmmmmmmmmmmmmm.*

Then the bell rang, and Seth kind of stepped away from me slowly, but turned so his arm was still over my shoulder. He scooped up his backpack as we walked toward class, and I worked at getting the goofy grin off my face before algebra.

Then I screeched to a stop and quit smiling. "Does this mean you're over your, um, issues with my, er, stuff?"

Seth had a weird look on his face for just a second; then he laughed and grabbed my hand and gently tugged till I started walking again. "Issues dealt with. How could I ever date a Normal again, after being with you?"

The part of me that was suspicious and insecure paused a moment; but then he smiled at me again and I could feel the big goofy grin spreading over my face for a second time. So I walked into algebra looking like a dork. Sadly, contentment—dorky or any other kind—never lasts long in my world.

"Hey, look—it's old orange head." Kelli's

snarkiness pierced my good mood less than—hey, new record!—thirty seconds later.

I sighed and shook my new and improved head of straight and no-longer-orange hair. "Sorry, Kelli. No orange here. You'll have to find a new victim."

Mr. Platt harrumphed a few times. "All right, girls. All right. Settle down. We need to talk about the results of yesterday's algebra quiz. Grading them almost turned *my* hair orange last night. It's pretty clear we're going to have to spend the entire class period reviewing what we've just learned. Pull out your books and turn to page one hundred and twenty-three."

I dropped into my chair and groaned. From kissing to algebra in five short minutes. Life was so unfair.

I caught up with Lily on the way to lunch, after an entire morning of being bored into a seriously mummylike trance. I'd almost felt my eyes rolling back in my head at one point in English, and managed to stay awake only because Mike poked me in the back with his pencil when I slumped backward. I winced and rubbed my shoulder. He could've at least used the eraser end.

"Jerk."

Lily looked down at me from her unfairly tall self and grinned. "Hey, who ya calling a jerk?" Then she got a good look at my face and frowned. "Who peed on your parade? Kelli get another jab in at you over the hair?"

I shook my head. "No, she almost doesn't bother me today, now that my hair is gloriously not—repeat, *not*,—orange, and after Seth . . . Um, oops. Never mind." I felt my face turn a little hot, and all I could think was how horrible a red face would've looked the day before, with my orange hair and all.

I shuddered.

Lily stopped in front of the cafeteria and waggled her finger in front of my nose, grinning. "Spill, Jessie, before I have to go ask Seth about it. I've known him since we were in diapers, so don't think I wouldn't."

I rolled my eyes and pushed past her into the cafeteria. "What*ever*. It was just a little hug before class. And maybe the teensiest kiss. No biggie."

"Right. No biggie. That's why you're glowing like a lit candle. I guess you solved whatever problem was bugging you guys?" She stopped to look at the posted menu and made a hideous face.

I read over her shoulder. " 'Creamed beef on toast'? What the heck is creamed beef? Is that a cow that somebody ran over with a car? 'Whoa, Betsy, I sure creamed that bovine. Let's slap it on some toast.' Where do they come up with this stuff?"

Lily was cracking up. She pointed to her lunch box. "I brought two sandwiches. No creamed anything; good old P-B-and-J. You can have one and I'll just get a snack later. You really need to start packing your lunch, J."

As we threaded our way through the tables to find a seat, I glanced at her over my shoulder. "You'll get a snack later? You mean you were going to eat both sandwiches? How are genetics so unfair?" I pointedly looked down at her yards-long, totally thin legs. "Will you please share some of your skinny DNA along with the P-B-and-J?"

She laughed. "Yeah, sure, *now* I'm thin. I'll probably pork up like my aunt Priscilla in my thirties and need a crane to get around."

I snickered at the idea of Lily waddling down Main Street (yeah, like that would ever happen) and snagged an empty table at the far side of the caf. As we sat down, the dark wind of doom blew over our table.

Kelli showed up.

"Oh, look at the losers eating their pathetic little sandwiches all by themselves. Doesn't it ever get to you, being such social outcasts?" She stood next to the table, hands on hips, with a fake-nice expression on her face, like she was asking how the weather was. Weirdly, none of her minions were flanking her. She usually never left home without them, so it was freaky to see her alone.

I raised one eyebrow. "Can we get you something, Kelli? A little creamed beef, maybe?"

Lily started laughing and almost choked on her sandwich.

Kelli narrowed her eyes and started to say something, then seemed to change her mind. Instead, she smiled at us again, almost in a pitying way, which creeped me out more than when she was being nasty. She walked to the other side of Lily and actually sat down.

At our table.

To get an idea of how bizarre this was, for head-cheerleader, popular Kelli to sit down at what she perceived to be the loser table, imagine the sun rising on the wrong side of the planet.

Yeah, *that* bizarre.

I knew that, whatever was going on, it was going to be bad. Enormondously bad.

Kelli tapped one long, acrylic, French-tipped nail on the table slowly, watching it as if it held the secrets to winning next summer's cheerleading all-state championship. Then she slowly raised her gaze and speared Lily with it.

"So I guess John hasn't told you yet, Lily," she said in an almost purring kind of tone. The hairs on the back of my neck stood up. It was going to be *really* bad.

Lily put her sandwich down on the table, all trace of her smile gone. "Told me what?" The ice in her voice would have scared off anybody with half a brain.

Quarter-brained Kelli wasn't fazed a bit. "That he's going away with me for the weekend. Don't worry; I'll have him back to you on Sunday." She stood up and brushed imaginary crumbs off of her way-too-short skirt and flicked a smug glance down at Lily.

"If, of course, he even wants to come back to you by then. Have a nice lunch, girls." She smirked one last smile at us and turned to saunter off, leaving us staring at her with our mouths hanging open.

I snapped mine shut first. "Lily, she's lying. She has to be lying. She's trying to make you crazy. Don't let her do it."

Lily shook her head slowly. "No, I've known Kelli all my life. I know when she's lying. She wasn't lying. How could he . . . what . . . ." Her eyes filled with tears, and she ducked her head.

I handed her my napkin and lowered my voice—not that anyone was around to hear, but still. "Look, we have to go find John right now and figure out what's going on, Lily. You can't put up with this crap from her. You have to fight for him."

Lily shook her head, then sniffled a bit and wiped her face. "No way. I won't give her the satisfaction. If he's really that stupid, he deserves her." She looked down at the mangled remains of her sandwich that she'd smashed as Kelli'd walked away.

"Suddenly I'm not hungry anymore. I'll catch up to you in biology, Jessie."

As Lily shot out of the cafeteria, I realized that this was twice that Kelli's plotting had made Lily lose her appetite. I narrowed my eyes and stared at Kelli where she was sitting with her minions and cheerleader wannabes. The wench was going down.

Mom and E were both standing on the front porch, waiting for me, when Seth dropped me off after school. I'd managed to fill him in on the trials, and he at least seemed interested and not hyper-spazzed about it. *So that's progress, right?*

I'm totally not going to kiss my boyfriend in

front of my mother and grandmother, so that was a bummer. Plus, if they were waiting for me on the porch, it had to be bad.

My heart sank down to a place somewhere around the button on the top of my low-rise jeans. "See you, Seth. Big powwow about important superhero stuff, I guess." I flashed a glance at him, to see if the SH thing bothered him.

He didn't look at me, just sort of squirmed in his seat, then said, "Right. See you later, then. I'll call you."

He still didn't look up as I got out of the car, so I figured that his "I'm over it" really meant, "I'm *trying* to be over it."

I dragged my feet up the sidewalk, staring at the ground. *So not in the mood for this.* Plus, now that I was home, I couldn't keep the League's last message from spinning around in my brain anymore: . . . *be removed from your home and fostered with a council member for the duration of your training, for a time period to be no longer than five years.*

Jerks. No way would Mom let that happen.

Would she? I looked up at her, all folded arms and frowny on the porch.

Five years wasn't that long, was it?

Aaarghhhh.

"Jessie! We need to talk. Please come in here

immediately," Mom said, then turned and disappeared inside the house.

E stayed on the porch and watched me move at the speed of an algebra review class toward the porch. "What's wrong, honey? Boy trouble? School trouble? Anybody I need to beat up for you?"

I started laughing. "Yeah, like I need my grandma to beat somebody up for me. That would cinch my rep as Skyville High Loser of the Year for all time, wouldn't it?"

She grinned and put an arm around my shoulders as we went inside. "Made you laugh, though, didn't I? And don't call me Grandma."

Mom called out from the kitchen: "In here, please. Now." The chill in her voice pretty much made the air-conditioning unnecessary. E and I looked at each other, the grins fading off of our faces.

"What is it?" I whispered.

"Bad news. Council," she whispered back.

Oh. That. They must have told Mom the same news about the fostering. I could feel tears starting to well up again and forced them away. "No use borrowing trouble," as Dad used to say.

Mom would know what to do.

I took a deep breath and walked into the kitchen. Mom sat at the table, head in her hands. She looked up at me, and I could tell she'd been crying.

"Jessie, I don't know what to do."

SuperJessie@Leagueblog.com

Okay, League creeps, you'd better watch out. You made my mother cry. (I know, I know, before you even say it, I made her cry this week, too, but that's different. That was normal teenage-crisis stuff, not "we're going to take your kid away from you" stuff.) My mom's had a tough time. First she lost Dad—and I know you guys had a lot to do with that, but we'll have that little talk when I'm old enough to do something about it—and now you're threatening to take me away if I don't pass your stupid trials.

Well, let me tell you something. There are laws in this country. I'm a free citizen and an American, and I didn't read anything in the Declaration of Independence that said "life, liberty, and the pursuit of happiness, except for sixteen-year-old superheroes." So you'd better watch out. Mom stood up for me and said she'd fight you and there's no way you're taking me away, but E said you had judis . . . jurdis . . . jurisdiction, whatever that means. But I was so happy that Mom was sticking up for me that I had to hug her. And we laughed about how the three of us could take Drake the Dork, even if he is the size of Godzilla. (Then stupid Luke called and Mom took off to talk to him, but it's not like she was abandoning me in my time of need or anything. Much. But that's none of your business, either.)

I'll pass your stupid trials, and then you can stay out of my life. I don't want anything to do with your sucky League of Liberty. And if you ever make my mom cry again, you'll answer to me.

So *totally not* yours,
Jessica Drummond

-11-

BROKEN CARS AND BROKEN HEARTS

I stepped off the bus (yeah, I was desperate this morning and not in the mood to walk two miles) in front of the school and stood there staring at the gym with about three hundred other people. Or, at least, at what was *left* of the gym. Okay, maybe that was exaggerating, but one small section of the front wall was kind of black and smoking, and firefighters, teachers, and lots and lots of grown-ups were huddled in little groups, talking. I scanned the scene for Ms. True and saw her with the fire chief.

Seemed like a good time for some superhearing action to me.

I narrowed my eyes, focused, and channeled.

". . . all that bad. It almost looks like a prank, rather than serious arson. Although, if Mike hadn't caught it in time, it certainly could have spread and caused some major damage." The fire chief sounded grim.

Mike again. What was it Avielle said? Paint thinner?

I focused again. Ms. True was talking. "Yes, if he hadn't stopped by to get an extra run in on the track, I don't know what might have happened. Thank goodness he saw the smoke coming out from under the door and had the presence of mind to call nine-one-one."

"Right. Thank goodness," I muttered, then jerked as somebody bumped my arm.

"Thank goodness what?" It was Mike.

I narrowed my eyes and stared right into his, trying to read his soul, like they say in books. (It doesn't work for me; I just saw eyeballs.)

I quit staring at him and shook my head. "Thank goodness the whole school isn't burned down. I'd *hate* to miss algebra."

He laughed and then ducked his head modestly, like "aw, shucks." "I'm just glad I decided to take that extra run and saw the smoke. The fire department got here before there was any real damage, I guess."

I pretended to be surprised. "Oh, it was you who called nine-one-one? That's great. Um, but why did you come clear back out here to run, when your family has that nice running track out in back around your tennis courts?"

(Mike's family had big bucks and didn't mind showing it off; the running track was right next to the pool. Rough life, huh?)

He looked at me kinda funny, then laughed again. "Oh, you know. Regulation track and all that. Hey, gotta get moving or we'll be late for your favorite subject. And isn't tonight your next driving lesson?"

I'd been really getting into my Ace Girl Detective thing, but the reminder of driving lessons with Mr. Platt froze me in my tracks. I willed myself to calm down. It had to be better than last time, right?

Right?

"Jessie, are you out of your *mind*?" Mr. Platt yelled at me, as I plowed over the fifth of the five cones set up in the middle of the parking lot. For the second time in a row.

In my defense, they were totally too close together.

I stepped on the brakes, remembering to press gently this time, and sighed. I crossed my arms on the steering wheel and rested my head on them, already knowing what was coming next: the "Jessie is the worst driver in the history of the universe, and I need to get out of this job" rant.

Mr. Platt didn't disappoint me. Again with the crazed muttering.

"Every year there's one. Always one who drives me to the brink of insanity. Not bad enough that there are mad arsonists running around setting fires in the school, but I have to take my life into my hands every day teaching insane teenagers how to drive. My brother said I'm too old for smoke jumping. Can you believe it? Like he's a spring chicken at forty-five. Mom always liked him better, anyway."

He speared me with a wild-eyed look. "You! You are the worst driver in the history of the universe. How can you possibly hit every single cone? Not just bump them or graze them or nudge them. Oh, no. Not you. You . . . you . . . you demolished them! The law of averages says that there's no way you could randomly plow into every single one of those cones, unless you were deliberately aiming for them. But your aim is so bad, that can't be it, either."

Hey! This is getting a little personal! I don't have to take this, do I?

Just as I opened my mouth to defend myself, Mr. Platt sighed a long, drawn-out sigh that sounded like he was blowing out half the air in Florida. Then he dropped his head to his chest and mumbled something.

"I'm sorry, Mr. Platt, what was that?"

He gave me such a desperate look, it reminded me of how I'd felt the time Chloe was only two, and she'd flushed my brand-new running watch down the toilet.

Mr. Platt tried again. "Flushed."

I whipped my head around to stare at him. *Whoa. That was weird. Is Mr. Platt psychic? Maybe a secret superhero sent by the League to spy on me? What if—*

"My career is flushed down the toilet."

Oh, his career, not my watch.

"Look, can't I just try again? I mean, it was so nice of you to let us use your nice new car for the lesson since the Ugly Mobile, er, I mean, station wagon, is in the shop. Your nice new car with the great brakes and, look, even the cute little air bags, so it's not like you can get hurt by a little cone or anything. Please, Mr. Platt, I'll hop out and put the cones back in place and try again. I'm sure I'll make it this time. You know, third time's a charm and all that. Right?" I tried my best to sound perky and hopeful.

Mr. Platt slumped even farther down in the passenger seat. He didn't look perky or hopeful. "No."

"No? But, Mr. Platt, I promise—"

"No. I mean, no, you don't have to put the cones back. The other students already did it. Just try again. And, Jessie, this is it. This is your last chance. My heart can't take any more." He made this weird moaning noise, then braced himself against the dashboard, arms locked in place, and squinted his eyes till they were almost shut.

"Go."

I straightened in the seat and gripped the steering wheel hard.

This is it. This is my big chance. I can prove I'm not a total weenie at this driving thing.

I took a deep breath, put my foot on the brake, and moved the gearshift thingy to D.

Foot on the gas pedal—gently, gently! Can't take off at eighty miles an hour like last time. Okay, way to go, Jess, made it around the first cone; didn't even touch it. Yeah! I can do this, I can do this. Calm down, calm down, slow down, you're pushing on the gas too hard, okay, that's it. Slow and steady around the next cone. Here it comes, left, left, just a little more, yeah! That's two down. I can so totally do this. I can do this and I can blast through those stupid trials. Who needs the League of Liberty, anyway? Bunch of losers! I mean, oops! Slow down, slow down, don't make Mr. Platt gasp any more. Gasping is bad, bad, bad.

Gently, gently, all right, turn to the right and smoothly around it, yes! I rock at this! Three down, and two to go. Not only am I gonna blast them out of the water in the trials, but I'm going to find out who's playing firestarter with my school. Okay, a little more to the left, a little more, remember this car wiggles on a hard left, I can do this, I can do this.

Awesome! I did it. Four down, only one to go; no way am I going to blow this. Like I need one more thing for Kelli to make fun of me about, since she already has her driver's license, with her private lessons and her stupid convertible, not that I would mind having a convertible, but I'll be lucky to get to drive the Bug and, oh, great, as if thinking her name brings her to life like some kind of pom-pom demon, there's Kelli with her stupid cheerleader outfit on, like boys really fall for that. Okay, they do actually fall for it and what are we going to do about John and poor Lily and I just have to make this turn and

do the very last cone before Mr. Platt has some
kind of cardiac arrest and that's . . . No, that's
Seth; what is he doing here and what is she . . .
What is Kelli doing touching my boyfriend, *get*
your hands off of him, you, you, you . . .

It was Kelli's fault. Totally.

She put her skanky hands on my boyfriend's
arm, and seeing it made me squeeze the steering wheel so hard that it really wasn't my fault
that it broke a little.

Shattered, I guess you might say. Kinda
pushed into the dash, even. *Oops.*

"Help! Jessie, watch out, hit the brakes, *aar-*
rrmmmmmpphhhh!"

I slammed on the brakes, then tried to look at
Mr. Platt to check that he was all right, but it's
kind of hard to see around an exploding air
bag. I guess pushing the steering wheel a couple of inches into the actual dashboard sets off
both air bags. Who knew? From the sounds of
the gurgling and choking going on over there,
it was kind of hard to talk with a mouthful of
air bag, too. I shoved at my own air bag, trying
to push it out of my way, and coughed from the
powder up my nose.

But, hey, it's not like I hit the cone!

The cone! I didn't hit it. The air bag thing
wasn't really my fault, since the car I was used
to didn't have air bags, right? Mr. Platt said I

had to finish the slalom course without hitting a single cone to pass today, and I didn't hit that cone! I was still in the running. Or in the driving. Or whatever.

"Mr. Platt, I know it's just a teensy bit uncomfortable, but hang on. I have one more cone to get around, and I'm going to do it. Just hang on."

Mr. Platt said something that sounded like "Eccky goorrpa roogggum," but, since I had no idea what that meant (maybe the teensiest idea, but no way was I stopping now), I put my foot back on the gas pedal, gently, and tried not to suck yucky air-bag powder in through my nose or mouth. I could hear everybody in the parking lot yelling, and the yelling kept getting closer, but I didn't have time for minor details. I squinted my eyes and focused and . . . yep, there it was . . . three cheers for X-ray vision! I could see right through the air bag blocking my view of the parking lot and the last, single, solitary cone left between me and my continued path to my driver's license.

Three, two, one, yes!

I braked and shoved the gearshift thingy into park and tried to punch my fist in the air, but the air bag kind of got in the way. Then there was big yelling, and banging on my window, and Seth yanked my door open and pulled me out of the car.

He kept hugging me and then peering at my face and kind of patting my arms all over. "Jess, are you okay? Why did the car keep moving? What happened? The air bag must be defective. Oh, Jessie, you scared me to death. If something happened to you, I—"

He took a deep, shuddery breath, and I could tell he really had been mondo worried about me. Which made what I had to tell him even worse. I hugged him back, closed my eyes, and whispered in his ear, "Um, Seth? It was kind of my fault. I broke the steering wheel when I saw Kelli hanging all over you. I'm so sorry; it was just a crazy reaction, and—"

He grabbed my shoulders and shoved me out to arm's length away from him, looking at me like I was some kind of psycho. "You what? You *what?*" Then he looked around and over at the people helping Mr. Platt out of the car and lowered his voice, but he sounded all rough and flustered and not like himself at all. "Other girls get jealous, they break dishes. *My* girlfriend gets jealous, she breaks a car."

Seth let go of my arms and let out a huge breath. "I just can't deal, Jess. I'm sorry. I need a break."

As some of the other kids helped Mr. Platt, still babbling about early retirement, across the parking lot, I tried to say something. Anything.

But for the first time in my life I was totally speechless.

Then, right there in the parking lot, next to the car I'd broken, and only three days before my birthday, I watched my boyfriend walk away from me and out of my life.

-12-

PAIN AND DR. PAYNE

-12-

PAIN AND DR. PAYNE

Slumped down in the corner of the passenger seat of the sheriff's car, I prayed for about the millionth time that nobody I knew would see me. "I still don't get why *you* have to take me to the orthodontist. Where's Mom?"

Luke made a gritting sound, like he was clenching his teeth, but his voice was pleasant enough. "As I said before, she had to take Chloe to sign up for dance classes. Since it's on my way, I said I'd be glad to take you to the orthodontist."

I rolled my eyes. "On your way. Isn't everything, like, on your way? I mean, all you do is cruise around in your car all day, right? It's not like Skyville has any desperate criminals for you to chase. This isn't New York or even Seattle, after all."

I sneaked a look at him and, judging from his white knuckles, he was clenching his hands on the steering wheel. (Good thing *he* didn't have to worry about superstrength.)

He laughed a little. "Nope, you're right. Not New York. I used to be a cop in Chicago, though, and I'm more than happy to be right here in peaceful little Skyville."

I thought about that for a minute. "What about the arson at the school? Why haven't you solved that, if you used to be Mr. Big-city Cop? Too busy trying to take up all my mom's time, huh?"

The sad part was that I could hear the brattiness in my voice, but I didn't seem to be able to stop it. The final straw had been Mom taking his call last night when we were talking about how to keep me out of the League's evil clutches. I mean, moms should have priorities. Dating sheriffs is not one of them.

Right?

I stared glumly at all the gadgets hooked up to the dashboard of the police car. *Hey, I wonder which button makes the siren and lights go off? That would at least be fun. Maybe . . .*

"Jessie. We should probably talk. I think—"

I turned my head to stare out the window and saw Dr. Payne's office building. Saved by the psycho orthodontist.

"Stop! We're here." I jumped out of the car before it even came to a complete stop and slammed the door behind me, then turned around to peer in at Luke, who looked a little confused. "No need to wait for me. I'll find my way home, no problem. Um, thanks for the ride and all."

Ha. That was polite. Nobody can say I'm not polite.

I rushed up the sidewalk to Dr. Lunatic's office, thinking about how weird it was that I was actually in a hurry to see her. Anything to get away from Luke and his "talk." I was practically running by the time I pushed the door open into the lobby.

And screeched to a stop.

Somebody was screaming.

This wasn't "Oh, ouch, that hurt" kind of screaming. It was more like, "Stop! You're killing me! I'm going to die any second!" kind of screaming. I'd unfrozen my feet from the ground and started to turn around to head right back out when the dental tech caught sight of me. "Hello, Jessie; we've been waiting for you. I'm Sandi. Come right on back."

I started stuttering out some kind of excuse, but Sandi laughed and walked up to take my arm. "Oh, don't mind the noise. That's Dennis. He has a bit of an emotional reaction at each of his appointments. His mother really needs to fill that sedative prescription Dr. Payne gave her." She made a *tut-tut* noise and started making her way back to the exam rooms, dragging me behind her. I was so freaked out by the screaming that it never occurred to me to turn on my superstrength and put up a fight.

Plus, we've all seen where superstrength has been getting me lately.

I plunged into a deep gloom, thinking about Seth, and let Sandi drag me along to my impending doom. As we passed exam room two, a skinny boy who looked a couple of years younger than me ran out and almost knocked me over. He stared at me, tears rolling down his face, and said, "Oga garm fargets! Elppee!"

Or, you know, something that sounded like that. Talk about a day when I practically needed a translator. First Mr. Platt and now this kid.

But I couldn't even focus on what he'd said, because I caught sight of his mouth. His totally terrifying mouth, stuffed with so much metal he couldn't even close his lips together. He also had a weird kind of metal headband thingy attached to his teeth armor—I guess they were *braces?* It looked like the kind of thing people who'd been smashed up in car accidents wear.

He yelled something else in gibberish at me, then made a break for the door. I stared after him, freaked out of my mind.

Gross. No way she's doing that to me.

Just then, Dr. Demented came out of the exam room. She saw me and actually rubbed her hands together, like a comic-book villain. "Oh, I'm glad you met Dennis, Jessie. That's the same type of braces and mouthgear we're going to put on you. There's going to have to be some drilling first, though."

She grinned her most despicably hideous grin. "Lots and lots of drilling."

"No way am I going back to that psycho! I can't believe you would even try to make me! After I told you and told you what a mental case she is, how could you send me there? With Sheriff Luke, no less? You don't even care about me enough to take me yourself?" I glared at Mom, who'd just had the nerve to tell me that I was, in fact, going to get braces on the day before my birthday.

She paced back and forth across the living room. "Jessie, you know you have a tendency to exaggerate. And hush, you'll wake up Chloe."

"Right. You waited all evening, until after Chloe was in bed, to have this discussion. That way you can say, 'Be quiet, Jessie.' 'Shut up, Jessie.' 'Too bad I'm going to ruin your life, Jessie.'"

I looked at her, feeling like my head was going to explode any minute. "Mom, do you really think I need help in the 'ruin my life' department? Let's see. My boyfriend just dumped me, because he can't handle having a superhero girlfriend. I broke the driver's-ed car, except it wasn't even the driver's-ed car; it was Mr. Platt's own personal car, so he'll probably flunk me in both driver's ed *and* algebra, to get even. Some escaped mental patient is masquerading as my orthodontist, and you care more about stupid Sheriff Luke than you do about me. Really, Mom, how could my life *be* any more ruined?"

Mom made a weird, strangly noise and pointed to something behind me. I whipped my head around to see what was there.

Make that *who* was there.

Sheriff Luke stood in the doorway, one hand on the door, with an enormondously freaked-out look on his face and his mouth hanging open.

Oh, crap. What did he hear? What did he hear?

139

-13-

TWO MISTERS PLATT

Whoever came up with the expression "a cold silence" should've been at my house for breakfast. It felt like winter at the North Pole. Mom didn't say a single word to me until after Chloe's friend Phoebe and Phoebe's dad came to pick Chloe up for school. Then she turned to face me, wiping her hands on a dishcloth, and spoke in a very quiet voice. "I told Luke I can't see him anymore, Jessie. We were lucky he didn't hear the part of your outburst about superheroes, as it is. If my dating Luke is going to cause this huge rift between you and me, then I won't date him. It's that simple. Please come straight home after school, so we can practice for your trials."

Then she carefully hung the towel on the edge of the dish rack and walked out of the room, without saying another word, while I stared after her in shock.

I looked down at my big bowl of cereal and bananas, which suddenly seemed pretty unappetizing. I'd gotten exactly what I wanted, right?

So when does the happy part kick in?

When Seth saw me walking toward him, he made a big point to walk the other way. This didn't help with the good mood, especially when I was on the way to algebra. Of course, Seth was on his way there, too, so I was going to have to face him at some point. I slowed my steps, hoping to get to class right as the bell rang, to avoid any chance for awkward conversation.

Especially conversation that somebody else might hear, like Mr. Platt or—

Oh, crap. Mr. Platt.

With all the other torture in my life, I'd managed to put the driver's-ed incident clear out of my mind. A psychotic orthodontist will do that to a girl. Not to mention the battle with Mom. I still couldn't believe she broke up with Luke because of me.

But now I had to face Mr. Platt, after I'd wrecked his new car. I considered going to the nurse to try the get-out-of-class trick again, but realized it would only get worse the longer I put it off. Facing up to my mistakes was getting to be a daily habit.

New T-shirt slogan: *Just Stay in Bed.*

I peeked around the corner of the doorway to judge how angry Mr. Platt looked before I completely ruled out the nurse thing. But he wasn't there. Some totally cute, totally tall, totally young guy leaned on the edge of Mr. Platt's desk. I took a step and peered around the room. No Mr. Platt anywhere.

Tall, cute guy spoke up. "Come on in, you're in the right place. Mr. Platt's taking the week off. I'm the substitute."

Waves of relief washed over me, and then waves of guilt did a backsplash in my conscience. "Um, is he . . . okay? Is his car going to be okay?"

The sub jerked his head up from where he'd been looking at our algebra book and stared at me intently. "Oh. You must be Jessie. Yes, he's going to be fine with a little rest and calm. Lots of calm."

Great. I'm a legend of klutziness even among the hottie substitute teachers, now. At least Mr. Platt is okay.

I felt my face getting warm. "Um, yeah. I'll just . . . go take my seat."

But walking down the aisle and away from him didn't make life suddenly all peachy. If anything, it got worse. First, the whispery snarking started.

". . . you hear what she did to poor Platt? Heard he'd be lucky to recover . . ."

". . . his heart, you know. She went psycho in the parking lot . . ."

". . . air bag . . . kept going . . ."

Then the not-so-whispery snarking. Kelli, of course.

"So, Jessie, first you drive Mr. Platt insane—ha, ha, *drive*, get it?" She actually waited for the laugh before going on. "Then I hear little Sethie dumped you. Can't even keep the math geek interested, hmmmm? That really is pathetic." She shook her head in mock sorrow.

I took my seat behind her, fantasizing about choking her with her own necklace. Then I noticed Lily trying to tell me something, but I just shook my head. I couldn't take any sympathy right then, or I was going to lose it. I made a point of not turning to look at Seth, either, no matter how much I wanted to sneak a peek to see if he was looking at me.

Mr. Substitute wrote something on the board

and turned around, wiping chalk off his fingers. I flicked a glance at what he wrote, as if I really cared the teensiest bit about algebra at a time like this.

Mr. Platt

Duh. Like we didn't know this was Mr. Platt's class by now. I decided to help out clueless boy.

I raised my hand. "Um, yeah, we know this is Mr. Platt's class. But what's your name?"

He looked at me kinda funny. "Mr. Platt."

I mentally rolled my eyes (which is harder than it sounds) and decided to speak slowly so maybe he could catch on. "Right. Mis. Ter. Platt. We. Under. Stand. That. But who are *you?*"

Sheesh, the guy was as thick as he was cute.

He grinned at me, which was unfair, 'cause he was way too cute to be a teacher. "I. Am. Also. Mr. Platt. Your. Mr. Platt. Is. My. Dad."

Oh, crap.

Somehow I made it to lunch, in spite of being talked about, pointed at, and laughed at everywhere I went. Not to mention the whole two-Misters-Platt disaster. I cringed just thinking about it. Of course, the smell of burned tuna melt may have had something to do with the cringing, too.

I'd tried to catch up to Seth in the hall, but he just said, "Not yet," and walked away. So I wasn't really in the greatest of moods when Lily rushed up to me.

"I can't believe it. I can't believe he's going to go to Disney with that wench. If he loved me, he wouldn't go," she said, looking like she wanted to hit something. I switched my brown bag lunch to the hand farthest from her, remembering the destruction of her innocent P-B-and-J.

"Lily, you have to tell him. Tell him what she said, and what she's planning, and that you don't want him to go," I said in a—to my mind, at least—reasonable tone.

"Jessie, that's completely unreasonable!"

I sighed. *Wrong again.*

I waited till we'd found a table and sat down, then made sure nobody was paying attention to us. (Well, other than everybody who was pointing and laughing and saying the words "Mr. Platt" over and over, which was apparently going to be my personal torture for the rest of my natural life.)

Then I unpacked my lunch and sort of blocked it with my body, since I like tuna-salad sandwiches the way Mom makes them and wanted to save this one, and took a deep breath.

"Lily, you have to tell him. It's not fair for you to expect him to read your mind or to read

Kelli's mind. He's a guy. All he sees is a free trip to Disney with his buddies."

She looked at me like I'd lost my mind. "No way. No way, no way, no way. If I have to tell him not to go, then we don't have much of a relationship, do we?"

"That's not true. You—"

Just then a couple of the Chess Club geeks walked by, including Miss Likes to Hug Other Girls' Boyfriends. They sneered at me as they passed and started talking really loud, like they wanted me to be sure to hear them.

"Did you know she drove Mr. Platt insane, and he had to go to a mental institution? I guess his son is here for revenge against her."

Miss Boyfriend Hugger snickered. "Yeah, no wonder she can't hold on to Seth. He needs a nice, normal, *sane* girlfriend."

I started to lunge up off the bench to go for her throat, but Lily grabbed my arm and tugged me back down. "Focus, Jess. Ignore those stupid girls and help me figure out what to do about John."

I bared my teeth at the sniggering creeps and then whipped around to face Lily. "For Pete's sake, Lily, could you just grow up? Can't you see I'm dealing with everything in my life falling apart here? You keep whining about John, but

146

you're not even brave enough to tell him what's going on. Just tell him. Or don't tell him. I don't even care anymore. I'm just tired of hearing about it."

The words had come rushing out of my mouth in a torrent, before I'd had a chance to think about what I was saying. But it was too late. The look on Lily's face said she might never, ever forgive me.

Oh, no.

"Lily, I—"

She jerked away from the arm I'd reached out to her and stood up. "Forget it, Jessie. I don't want to bother you with my petty little problems. I think I'll just go find someone else to talk to while I *grow up.*"

Then she ran out of the caf, and I sat there watching tears fall on my tuna sandwich, wondering just when and how I'd turned into the worst person in the universe.

The worst person in the universe didn't have much of a chance of passing her trials at the League Saturday, I figured. It's just a karma thing. So I wasn't exactly moping, as much as just being realistic, when E put me through some tests at home.

That's not how she saw it, though.

"Jessica Drummond! I expect more of you than this. Do you *want* to wind up fostered with some arrogant council member?"

I tossed the four-hundred-pound steel bar on the ground. *Oops. That made a big hole.*

"Look, E, I'm doing my best. But my best is never good enough, is it? Everybody in Skyville hates me, anyway. I may as well just leave town." I tore the eye mask off my face.

"I'm sorry I can't use my X-ray vision and superstrength both perfectly at the same time you're pointing that horrible noisemaker at me. Sure you don't want to make me run a few hundred miles, while you're at it? Facing the League trials can't be nearly as tough as this." I wiped my face with my sleeve, which didn't help much, since both were soaked with sweat.

Even superheroes sweat in Florida.

E folded her arms and gave me her calm, "I'm in charge" stare. "Fine. If you're done feeling sorry for yourself, we'll start over."

"But—"

"I said, we'll start over."

We started over.

Two hours later, even E was ready to give up. I just couldn't do it. Every time I managed to control one, then two powers at the same time, I'd think about how I'd made a mess of everything.

148

About how I'd hurt Mom and made her break up with Luke. About Lily's face when I'd told her to grow up.

About Seth saying he just couldn't deal.

Then I'd fail. Again and again and again.

E sighed from where she'd slumped down on the porch steps about an hour earlier. "I just don't know what's blocking you, Jessie. I wish you'd talk to me. I wish you'd talk to your mother. Something. There's no way you're going to be able to pass the trials like this. We're out of time."

I just shook my head. I didn't know where to begin. Then, suddenly, I did, and the words came pouring out.

"I'm just messing everything up, E. I hurt Mom's feelings, and I hurt my best friend, and I'm too stupid to pass driver's ed or even algebra, and my boyfriend said he can't deal with me being a superhero. My first boyfriend ever, and I really trusted him and really, really liked him—I still like him—and he already knew about us being superheroes, but he still can't deal. Just when I thought my future as a kiss virgin was gone forever, I find out that I'll be a one-kiss wonder."

I took a deep, shuddery breath. "Well, maybe more than one, but only ever one guy, and he doesn't even like me anymore. If I can't make it work with Seth, what chance do I have of ever getting a Normal guy to like me? I mean, a *normal* Normal guy who doesn't know about us. Maybe it's better that I fail my trials. Maybe it's better that I get taken away. Mom could go back to dating Luke and everybody would be better off." I laughed a little. "Mr. Platt would be better off, for sure, poor guy. The old one, not the young one."

As I stood there fighting to keep from sobbing, the back door banged open. Mom stood there for a second, her fist to her mouth; then she vaulted down the steps and ran across the yard and grabbed me in a fierce hug.

"Oh, baby. Don't you ever, *ever* think that I'd be better off without you. You are my darling girl, my first baby, my sweet pumpkin. I love you, Jess. I love you. We're going to figure this out together."

I hugged her back so hard and burst into tears. "I love you, too, Mom. I'm so sorry. I don't know what's wrong with me these days. Sometimes I feel like my head's gonna explode. I'm so sorry. I love you, too."

We just stood there hugging and snuffling for a few minutes, and then E spoke up, sounding amused. "All right. If the girly tearfest is over, maybe we could go make some dinner? I have a few stories to tell you about exploding heads and your mom turning sixteen, Jessie." She grinned and turned to walk inside.

I laughed, and then Mom and I started to follow E in the house. Suddenly I stopped. "Oh, and Mom?"

"Yes, dear?"

"Please don't ever, ever call me your sweet pumpkin in front of my friends."

Mom laughed and swatted at me, but I ran inside. All the same problems still hung over my head, but it was the best I'd felt all week.

Lives4Art@skyvillenet.com says:
I hope you're proud of yourself. I talked to John and he thinks I'm being a wacked-out, jealous nutcase. We yelled at each other, and we broke up. So, hey. I guess I'm grown-up now. Lily, your ex-best friend.

DramaQueen@skyvillenet.com says:
Way to go, Jessie. Lily was crying her eyes out. I guess this is how friends act in Seattle? Well, here in small-town Skyville, we care about people more than that. Avielle.

I fell asleep thinking: *One step forward, two steps back.*

-14-

DR. DEMENTED GOES BALLISTIC

Breakfast was much more cheerful on Friday morning, in spite of my impending doom at the orthodontist that afternoon. I'd tried to talk Mom out of making me go, saying that the stress from the whole thing would make me fail my trails for sure.

No dice. She was all, "No matter what else happens, you're going to have straight teeth."

Mothers. Who understands anything they do?

Anyway, I'd left early and wore comfortable ballet flats with my jeans, so I could walk to school and practice zoning and channeling on the way. No telling what kind of test the council would have cooked up for my superhearing.

Zone: Waves of sound, beginning with the animals having breakfast at the farm outside of town. (In case you ever wondered, pigs are noisy eaters. Euwwwww.)

Channel: *Who should I pick, who should I pick?* I tried never to channel in on my friends, because it seemed like sneaky eavesdropping. But I didn't have any problem with . . .

Mike.

". . . really big planned for tonight. It's going to be a night the school will never forget." He laughed, and it didn't sound like a very *nice* laugh. In fact, it gave me the creeps.

Somebody near Mike laughed, in a deep kind of grown-up voice. That laugh creeped me out, too. I could feel the little hairs on the back of my neck standing up (which was weird, since I'm not a dog, but still).

I channeled as hard as I'd ever channeled, but Mike didn't say anything else. I heard a car door slam and jumped, but there weren't any cars around me. It must have been Mike leaving for school. Was that his Dad? What were they talking about? What would the school never forget?

My rational side tried to speak up. *He's probably talking about the Disney trip. Mike's going on Kelli's evil little road trip, too.*

Luckily, I never paid much attention to my rational side.

Something inside me said that Mike had devious things in mind, and I needed to talk to—

Okay. Take a breath. Full stop. Who could I talk to?

Lily wasn't speaking to me. Avielle wasn't speaking to me. Seth didn't want to be around me. It's not like I could tell the new and improved Mr. Platt Junior that I'd tuned in to the star quarterback of the Skyville High football team and suspected him of planning something bad for tonight.

Besides, what bad thing could it even be?

Unless . . . *The paint thinner. Oh, man. What if Mike really is the Skyville arsonist?*

Rational Jessie spoke up again. (You had to admire her persistence.) *What possible reason would Mike have to set fires in the school? He's a sports star, he gets good grades, and he probably has scholarship offers rolling in. Not to mention he's rich. Why would he risk blowing it all?*

I didn't have any answer to that one, but my gut just said something was freaky. Since I usually listen to my gut way more than I listen to my head, I had to do something. Or tell someone.

But what? Or who?

* * *

"Seth!" He had to listen to me. He just *had* to.

"Jessie. I've been looking for you. We need to talk. I don't care if we're late for algebra; we need to talk now." He swiped his hair out of his eyes and grabbed my hand, then took off down the hallway. I was so freaked out, I let myself be dragged along, my thoughts speeding around in my head like a hamster on a wheel.

Whoa. Seth doesn't care if we're late for algebra? Has the world ended?

We took a turn and headed down the stairs.

Oh, crap. If he's willing to miss math, it has to be bad. He's had it. He wants a nice, Normal girlfriend.

I tried to be brave and think "I'm better off without him" thoughts as he pulled me into the gym. Better to be the dumper than the dumpee, right?

"Look, Seth Blanding, if you think you're going to make me late for algebra, which I happen to like now that Mr. Platt is there . . . well, the other Mr. Platt, not the first Mr. Platt, although how confusing is it to have two Misters Platt, anyway? And how weird that they're both math geeks . . . er, I mean, teachers, of course, they *are* related, and why are you stalking me like that?"

He just smiled and nudged me back a little more, until my back was against the gym door.

Then he walked up really, really close to me and smiled.

Oh, that is so totally the last straw!

"Look, I don't know what you're so happy about. If you think it's a fun time, the "Let's Dump Jessie" game, let me tell you that—Uuu-ummmmmmmmm."

Strange. Kissing's not usually part of dumping, is it? Is this a pity kiss? I think . . . Ummmm-mmmmmmm. So not thinking right now.

He stepped back and took a deep breath, then put a finger over my lips when I tried to talk. "I'm sorry, Jess. This was all my problem. *My* problem, not yours. I'm the one who had a tough time handling the superhero thing. You're funny and crazy and so nuts you drive *me* nuts, but anytime I think about not having you around, I get, you know, bummed out."

He stuffed his hands in his pockets and ducked his head. "I'm not going to go all girlie and talk about my feelings or anything, but, well, life without you was looking pretty lame. So if you can forgive my boneheadedness, I'd like another chance."

He's not dumping me? He's not dumping me! Even more important, he said he was sorry. That was a real-live apology.

Part of me—the part that maybe was getting

a little less insecure—realized that I deserved it. Just like Mom had deserved mine yesterday.

As Seth kissed me again (okay, I kissed him back, too), the warm glow of forgiveness spread through me. I figured that a few other people deserved apologies, too. From me, this time.

But Mike isn't one of them.

"Mike!" I almost yelled it.

Seth looked hurt. "Great, Jess. Yell Mike's name when I'm kissing you. Way to make a guy feel all warm and happy."

I gave him a quick hug. "No, silly. And yes. I mean, no, I'm yelling Mike's name because we have to figure out what he's up to, and yes, I forgive you. I could have been more understanding myself lately. But we seriously have to talk, now."

The bell rang just then, of course. There's never any "saved by the bell" in my life. More like "annoyed by the bell."

Seth looked at his watch. "We've gotta go. Let's talk after algebra. I'll meet you by your locker."

"Good plan." I turned to leave, and felt his hand on my shoulder.

"Not just yet, Jess." He kissed me again, and my stomach went all melty and gooshy. *This kissing thing is pretty cool.*

Yeah, your mom liked it, too. Too bad you messed that *up.*

I told my conscience to shut up. One thing at a time.

I could only fix one thing at a time.

Speaking of fixing things . . .

We started running up the stairs for class as the second bell rang. "Seth? I could use your help practicing for the trials."

He grabbed my hand and grinned at me. "I thought you'd never ask."

Lily and Avielle still weren't speaking to me, but I'd managed to pass notes to them in biology when Snoozebod, our ancient teacher, was droning on about DNA or something.

Hey—I'm sorry about everything. I've been a brat and I was totally wrong and U R the best friends I've ever had. But I promise 2 fix everything. U have 2 meet me at the gym at 8 P.M. tonight. Bring flashlights. Please! This is totally, ENORMONDOUSLY important!

Your friend 4-ever, Jessie (who's really, really sorry)

If that didn't work, nothing would. I was out of time, though. Now I had to face the worst moment of my entire life.

I had to go get braces.

* * *

Dr. Neurotic stared down at me, the spotlight shining directly in my eyes and her oniony breath washing over me. I was totally gonna yark any second, either from the breath or from the sheer terror of what I was about to face. My gaze skittered away from all the metal on the tray again. It looked like the prep table for somebody's dungeon of torture.

With the light in my eyes, though, I couldn't tell which one was in the room with me—Dr. Jekyll or Dentist Hyde?

Then she laughed. Cackled, really.

Answered that question.

I cringed as far back in the chair as I could get. Knowing Mom was in the waiting room gave me a boost of courage. She'd asked Phoebe's parents to keep Chloe overnight so she could stay with me, no matter how long it took, and then take care of me afterward.

She even promised me ice cream. With hot fudge.

(Not that I'm a total baby or anything, who needs to be bribed with ice cream, but come *on. Hot fudge.*)

Oops. Wandering. Psycho Doc was coming at me with something big, metal, and scary that made a terrible drilling sound. Like a drill, even.

Oh, no, not the drill.

"Just open up, Jessie. Open up and we'll drill

all those lovely, lovely teeth. Hee, hee, hee."
(She actually said the words "hee, hee, hee." It
was freakish.)

Then it got worse.

She burst into song.
"Drilling, drilling, into your teeth tonight.
We love to drill, we love to drill.
We love to make teeth right.
Drilling, drilling—"

All the time she sang, she shoved her drill
closer and closer to my face. Not *in* my mouth,
because my lips and teeth and entire mouth,
actually, were clamped shut in total horrified
paralysis. I could hear myself screaming, but it
was only in my head. *I may never, ever open
my mouth again. She has to get away from
me with that drill; she has to get away. No!
Not closer—get it away, get it away, Get it
away!*

The sound of the drill freaked me out completely, like a million bees buzzing inside my
skull. The sight of her insanely gleeful grin put
me over the edge.

She got closer. I cringed away.

She got closer and closer and closer. The arm
of the chair finally stopped me from backing
any farther away.

She must have lost patience, because then she yelled at me. "Open your mouth *right now!*"

So, technically, it was her fault for yelling.

The yelling put *me* over the edge. The scream that had been trapped in my head ripped its way out of my throat, getting louder and louder on its way out, until it sounded like the scream to end all screams and my mind was cracking and I was sure my ears were bleeding, and then—

Booommmm!

Oh, no! It was a lot like the air bag in the car! But . . . what did I explode this time?

Dr. Payne dropped her drill on the floor in shock as the explosion ripped through the room. We looked at each other, openmouthed, then looked around the room. Nothing was broken or damaged, or blown to bits, which was what it had sounded like.

The yelling started in the hallway, though. Dr. Drill ran out of the room just as Mom ran in.

"Jessie, are you all right?" She practically scooped me out of the chair in a hug. "I heard that noise, and I . . ."

She suddenly stopped hugging me and stared into my eyes. "Oh, Jessie. Oh, honey. Was it you? What did you do now?"

Before I could answer (and to be honest, I have no idea what I might have said), a weird howling noise shrieked in at us from what sounded like the exam room next door. Mom and I both flinched, then ran for the door.

What we saw was so awful, so hideous, so repulsive, that it may have traumatized my young self forever and ever.

Or at least for a few weeks.

My psychotic orthodontist was lying on the floor in a fetal position, arms wrapped around a big hunk of some metal machine, crying and stroking it.

"My poor baby, my poor compressor, my poor baby. You're all broken and now the lovely drills won't work, and I can't drill the nasty teenagers. Nasty, filthy teenagers with their nasty, filthy teeth. They all need drilling. All of them."

She looked up at Mom and me through tear-drenched eyes. "My poor, precious compressor. My poor baby. Somebody call nine-one-one. Get help. Get help for my poor baby."

Then she wrapped herself even more tightly around the broken machine (a compressor, I'm guessing) and started sobbing.

Mom looked at me, eyes bugging out and mouth hanging open. "You . . . She . . . Oh, God. Oh, Jessie. I'm so sorry I didn't believe you. Honey, I'll never doubt you again." She gave me a quick hug, then snapped into "Mom on a mission" mode, barking out orders for people to get back, move away, call 911, get an ambulance, and check Dr. Payne's address book to see if she had a psychiatrist they could call.

Nobody ever messes with Mom when she's barking orders, so everybody jumped to do what she said. I backed away from the room slowly, then faster and faster, 'cause the sight of Dr. Pitiful was suddenly way more than I could handle.

As I hung out in the lobby, waiting for the ambulance or people from the rubber-room palace to get there, I remembered what Mom had said. She'd apologized for not believing in me. I realized again, like I had with Seth in school, how wonderful an "I'm sorry" felt. I lifted my chin, remembering that I had some more "I'm sorrying" to do myself. It was totally my turn.

First, though, I had to do something just for me. I had to make sure I'd pass the trials.

Then I needed to call John.

-15-

Arsonists and Off Base

It was amazing how easy it was to pass all the tests that E could throw at me, when Seth was there rooting for me and helping me focus. Who knows more about focus than a math geek? I zoned, I channeled, I X-ray visioned, and I ran the four miles round-trip to the school in two and a half minutes.

For the final test, E pulled out all the stops. I had to stand on first one leg, then the other, holding that stupid picnic table overhead with not one, not two, not three, but *four* of the people I cared most about sitting on top of it.

Chloe leaned over the edge of the table and blew raspberries at me the whole time—*pffthh-hhh*—to test my concentration, while E kept switching that horrible buzzing machine on and off. The only near disaster, though, happened when Chloe started singing.

"Jessie and Seth sitting in a tree.
K-I-S-S-I-N-G.
First comes love—"

"Chloe! I'm going to drop you on your head if you don't stop it right now!" I felt the table jiggling wildly, as I tried not to think about how totally my annoying sister was embarrassing me.

Then Seth spoke up, sounding amused. "Hey, Jess. How about I kiss Chloe, since she likes to talk about kissing so much?"

Chloe shrieked, Mom and E laughed, and I relaxed.

I can do this. I can do this.

E thought so, too. "Jessica, you can do this. You're certainly going to be able to pass any trials the League council can throw at you. You can put us down now, dear. You're terrific!"

Mom said, "Jess, just let go. I've got it." So I did, and then moved out of the way while she floated the table back down to the ground.

Seth shook his head. "You guys are amazing. I

know the truth about superheroes and the League of Liberty, but it's still hard for me to deal, sometimes."

At the words "hard for me to deal," I froze. *Not again.*

"Seth?" I asked, in kind of a squeaky, quavery voice. "What do you mean by that?"

Seth grinned and jumped off the table. "I mean it's hard for me to deal with how lucky I am to be dating the prettiest superhero in Skyville."

E laughed. "Good save, young man."

I wasn't so impressed. I folded my arms and tapped my foot. "Only in Skyville?"

"All of Florida," he said.

"It's a small state," I pointed out.

"The entire United States, then?" he asked.

I shook my head, trying to keep a grin from quirking up the corners of my lips, as Mom and E herded Chloe inside to get ready for dinner. "Still not getting it, Blanding."

Seth swooped me up in a hug and swung me around. "You're right. The prettiest superhero in the entire universe. Now, if you've had enough flattery for one afternoon, what's up?"

The grin faded from my face. "Tonight we've got to go save the school from the arsonist."

After dinner Seth drove me to the neighborhood grocery store, located only a couple of blocks from the school. When we pulled into the parking lot the first person I saw was John. He was pretty ticked off, if the clenching and unclenching of fists meant anything. I looked at Seth and sighed. "Here goes."

He smiled at me. "You can do it, Jessie."

I nodded. "I've been hearing that a lot lately, and I think I'm starting to believe it. Let's go fix a relationship and catch a crook."

As we got out of the car, I could have sworn Seth said something like, "girls and relationships, bluck," but I didn't have my superhearing switched on, so I couldn't be sure. When I narrowed my eyes at him, he just gave me the "who, me?" face.

Hmmph. Making a note to deal with skeptical boys later, I marched over to John.

He scowled at me. "Hey, Jessie. This had better be good. I had to stuff things in my bag for the Disney trip, and I don't even know if I remembered underwear. I don't want to have to wear the same pair for three days, dude."

I could feel my face crinkle up in disgust. "Euuwwww! Can we just pretend you never, ever said something so disgusting and get on with the important part of the evening? I've got something to tell you both."

Seth had caught up with us by then. "What is it?"

"It's about the fires. I think I know who's starting them." I paused for effect, looking back and forth between them.

Boys aren't much for dramatic pauses, though. John blew out a breath. "So, get on with it. Who? And what do we have to do with it? Why didn't you call the police?"

I shook my head. "I don't have enough proof for the police. They need evidence, like on those TV shows. I should know; my mom is dating a sheriff. Or, at least, she *was* dating a sheriff before I messed it up. But I'm totally going to—"

"Jessie!" they both yelled at me at the same time. (Which is kind of unfair, but whatever.)

"Sorry. Brain ramble. It's Mike." I lifted my chin, proud of my detective abilities.

John tilted his head and looked all grossed out. "Mike is dating your mom? That's wacked, Jess."

"Euuwww! No, Mike isn't . . . That's just nasty! Sheriff Luke is . . . Oh, for Pete's sake. Mike is the *arsonist*. He's the one setting the fires. And we're going to catch him at it tonight."

Seth and John looked at each other, then at me. Then they both cracked up.

Seth recovered first. "Mike? Mike of the football team, richest family in Skyville, Mike? Sorry, Jess, but you're totally off base here. What possible reason could he have to set fires?"

John was laughing so hard, I thought he'd

rupture something, but then he had to chime in, too. "You're nuts. No way would Mike put his future in the toilet. We just had c-c-college scouts out to watch us last weekend. He has a chance to go big. No way, Jess. You're out of your mind. That orange hair dye must have f-f-fried your brain cells."

Then he started laughing again.

I'd had enough, though, way back at "fried." I punched him in the stomach, with maybe the teensiest bit of superstrength behind it.

He doubled over. "Oooomph. Hey! You pack a big punch for a little girl."

I waggled my finger in front of his face. "Don't call me a little girl, or I'll punch you again."

Seth broke in, grinning. "Don't worry, John; I won't let my girlfriend beat you up. But seriously, Jess, why would you think such a crazy thing? I'm assuming you do have reasons?"

John straightened up and backed away from me a skinch. "Yeah, why? This isn't some weird kind of revenge for how he treated you back before Mini Prom, is it?"

I rolled my eyes. *Boys.* "No, of course not. I'm so over that. Listen, I can't explain everything, but I happened to overhear some stuff that Mike said that sounded really suspicious. Avielle caught him buying paint thinner—highly flammable paint thinner—at the store. And that college scout you mentioned? Wasn't he just here to see *you?* Isn't it possible that Mike was a little jealous?"

I could almost see the brain cells working in John's and Seth's heads, they were thinking so hard. Then I caught sight of part two of my master plan: Avielle's car pulled into the parking lot.

With Lily inside.

I grabbed John's arms and pulled him around to face me, so he didn't see them yet. "Listen to me, John Bingham. There's something else you need to know. Something I heard straight from the horse's butt's mouth. Kelli planned this whole Disney trip thing to get you away from Lily, so she could put the moves on you."

His mouth dropped open, but I didn't have time to deal with questions. I plowed forward. "She told Lily that she was going to take you away from Lily, now that college scouts were looking at you and you were *important* enough for her. Lily didn't want to tell you, because she thought you should figure it out yourself. Lily trusts you."

I took a deep breath and finished in a hurry, because I could see Avielle trying to drag Lily out of the car, and Lily shaking her head no, no, no.

"I'm the one who kinda bullied Lily into confronting you. So if you're mad at anybody, be mad at me. Not Lily. She's crazy about you, and this whole thing really hurts her."

John stood there, his mouth opening and closing like a fish gasping for air. It wasn't pretty.

"I . . . she . . . I . . . really? Kelli's after me?" He grinned. "That would be kinda cool, if she wasn't the black widow of Skyville."

I just gaped at him. If anybody in the history of the world *ever* understands boys, I wish they'd write a book, 'cause I never, ever will.

John turned to give Seth a high five, which made me want to hit them both. *Must work on these anger-management issues. Next week, for sure.*

Then John saw Lily and Avielle and took off across the parking lot. I started to follow, but Seth grabbed my arm and held me back. "Let's let them figure it out, Jess. I think you've done the best you could. Now why don't you fill me in on the rest of the story about why you suspect Mike?"

As quickly as I could, I sketched in the details, including what I'd heard when I supereavesdropped. Seth quirked an eyebrow at that, but stayed silent. The whole time I was talking, I watched John and Lily.

First John talked, and Lily shook her head and stared at the ground in silence.

Then she talked, and he shut up.

They they both yelled at each other for about a minute and a half.

Then John swooped Lily up in a huge hug.

Then there was kissing. I just *love* it when a plan comes together!

Avielle, who'd been hiding out in her car during the fireworks, got out and rushed across the parking lot. She slowed down as she came close, but she was smiling. "Your handiwork?" she asked, pointing at Lily and John.

I just grinned and nodded.

"Good job," she said, and scuffed the toe of her shoe on the ground.

Seth rolled his eyes. "Oh, just do your girlie hug thing, and get it over with. We have to get over to the school."

Avielle and I both cracked up and grabbed each other in a huge hug. "I'm so sorry I was rude to Lily. It's been a horrible week, but that's no excuse to be rude to your friends, ever."

Avielle nodded and stepped back. "I'm sorry, too, Jessie. If you're having a tough time, I should have been there for you more. You just have to open up and let us know what's going on with you, okay?"

"Okay." I'd try. Really I would. It's just tough when the biggest thing on your mind is the one thing you can never talk about.

Seth must have known what was going on in my head, because he took my hand in his and gave it a gentle squeeze. I really like that guy.

Lily and John walked over to us just then, hand in hand. Lily gave me a slightly teary smile. "Okay, Jessie. I guess we have a firestarter to catch?"

I threw myself across the space between us and grabbed her in a big hug. "I'm so sorry, Lily. Please forgive me. I was being a total turd, and I'm so sorry."

Lily hugged me back hard. "I'm sorry, too. You're *not* a turd, and thank you for whatever you said to John."

Avielle threw her arms around both of us and we just stood there, laughing and crying in a big group hug, until John and Seth pulled us apart.

Seth grabbed my hand. "Look, this display of girl power is great and all, but don't we have somewhere to be? If only to prove that Mike is *not* the arsonist?"

Lily and Avielle both started talking at the same time. "What? Mike? What are you talking about?"

I took a deep breath. "I'll explain it all on the way. Right now we have to get over to the school and hide. Did you bring your flashlights? It's getting dark."

-16-

JESSIE SAVES THE DAY, BUT NOT EXACTLY THE CAR . . .

Everybody stuck with me, but I wasn't convinced that any of them believed me. Even Seth, who knew about what I'd overheard when I was channeling, was doubtful. He thought that Mike could have been talking about anything.

I had to admit that he had a point, but my gut said Mike was up to no good. Since guts aren't good enough evidence to take to the police, we were gonna stake out the school. Everybody was supposed to meet in the school parking lot at ten P.M. for the Disney trip, so we had about an hour to wait before the first people showed.

They'd planned such a late start so Kelli's dad could get back from some business trip in New York, I guess.

Lily must have been thinking about the Disney trip, too, 'cause she stopped walking and looked up at John. "Shouldn't you go get your stuff for your trip? I totally understand if you want to go have fun with your teammates, now that you know about Kelli."

John laughed and put his arm around Lily's shoulder. "No way, Lily. How about I stay here and we all go bowling and stuff ourselves on chili dogs, instead?"

Reunions are nice and all, but we had a job to do. "Come on, guys," I hissed. "We have to hide before Mike shows up."

John shook his head, but he and Lily started walking again.

"That's odd," said Seth.

"What?" I whipped my head around, looking for Mike or explosive devices or cans of paint thinner or something. Nope, didn't see anything.

Seth gently put his hands on both sides of my head and turned it to face the trees on the side of the road. There, pulled back in and mostly hidden by the trees, sat Luke's car. His sheriff's car.

Hmmmmm.

Seth made a worried face. "Jess, if the police are involved in this, we don't want to get in their way. That's obstruction, or something like that. We could get in big trouble. Plus, if this is dangerous, there's no way I want you to get hurt."

Doesn't it make you go a little gooey when boys get all protective?

I smiled and batted my eyelashes a little bit. "Oh, Seth, I'm safe with you." Then I turned serious. "Listen, even if it is the sheriff or a deputy, they don't know what they're looking for. Or *who*. We do, though. So we need to do this. If you guys want out, that's fine. But I'm staying."

I kept walking, trying really hard not to turn around and see if anybody was coming with me. Then I heard footsteps.

Lots of footsteps. I sneaked a peek. *Whew!*

Avielle stepped up beside me. "No way we're letting you go into this on your own. The Three Musketeers, right?"

Lily stepped up on the other side of me. "Right."

I could hear John muttering to Seth, just behind us. "What does that make us, the funny sidekicks?"

"Shhhhhh!" I cautioned. We were sticking to the shadows, but almost up to the school. "Quiet, now, in case they're here already. Let's get in place."

We split up and everybody sneaked off to

their designated waiting spots. I'd picked the outside wall of the cafeteria, since it was right in the middle of the two previous fires—the gym on one end of the school and Ms. True's office on the other. Plus, any fire would be seen really well from the parking lot when the kids and parents started arriving to catch the bus for Disney.

I scrunched down in the bushes and waited, wishing I'd thought of walkie-talkies or something.

I waited.

And waited.

And waited.

Bugs attacked me in swarms. (*Note to self: Carry bug spray for all future stakeouts.*)

Then I waited some more, sure I was going to die of boredom, the cramp in my leg, or itchiness.

I checked my watch for the thousandth time. Nine thirty-eight.

I must have been wrong. Everybody is going to show up any minute; they won't take a chance on getting caught.

I had started to stretch my legs out when I heard it.

Crunch.

A man's voice called out softly: "Hey, quiet! We're behind schedule as it is."

Another voice responded in a loud whisper. I

strained to hear. . . . It was Mike! "We're behind schedule because you forgot the matches and we had to stop and buy a lighter, Dad. This is stupid, anyway. I don't want to hurt the school."

It's his dad? What kind of dad does something like this?

The man snorted. "We're not hurting the school. We're making you a hero. We start a little fire; then you rush up, break the window, get the fire extinguisher, and put it out, all after you call nine-one-one on your cell phone. You're a hometown hero, and those college scouts will have to take that into account, instead of focusing all their attention on that muscle-brained Bingham."

I heard a splashing noise and smelled something really, really nasty. *Oh, crap. They're putting the catch-fire stuff on the wall! It smells like gas! What do I do now?*

In all my planning, I'd never thought about what to do if I actually caught them.

Oops.

Well, I had to do something. I couldn't just sit there and let them light the school on fire! Plus, they were close to splashing that firestarter stuff on my new Wet Seal tank top.

I stood up. *Ow! Charley horse in my leg!*

"Ow! My leg hurts! I mean, *stop!* You're in big trouble!"

Somebody switched a flashlight on in my face. "Who . . . Jessie? What are you doing here? Oh, man. This sucks."

"Mike, I know it's you. Get that light out of my eyes! You're in major trouble, buddy! You—"

Another voice broke in on my trembly speech. It was Sheriff Luke.

I adore that man.

"She's right. You're in major trouble. Step back and put that can of gasoline down. Where's the other one? I saw—*Uumphhh.*"

There'd been a loud whacking sound just before Sheriff Luke made that weird noise. I suddenly remembered my own flashlight.

And my voice.

I switched the flashlight on and started yelling as loud as I could: "Help! Help! Over here! It's Mike and his dad!"

I saw Luke's crumpled body on the ground. "Oh, no! Help! They've hurt Sheriff Luke! Help!"

Mike's dad yelled at him. "Come on, Mike. We have to get out of here! Run, run, *run!*"

Mike looked at me for a second. "Jess, I'm sorry. I just—"

"Yeah, I know what you *just*. But we caught

181

you. Your firebug days are over, dude. Probably your football career, too. Why would you DO this?"

Mike kinda looked mondo sad and glared at me all at the same time. "Dad thinks a big scholarship will attract more media attention and then that will attract the pro scouts. Football is his life, and all that crap."

He hesitated, and then threw down his flashlight and turned to run. I felt all mixed up and didn't know whether to be sorry for him or mad at him. I sucked in a deep breath and yelled after him, "Mike, don't run! It'll be worse if you run."

But he just kept going. Seth, Lily, John, and Avielle all appeared at the same time. "Jessie, are you hurt?"

"What happened?"

"We saw—"

I broke into the middle of it. "I'm fine, but I think Mike's dad hit Luke pretty hard with something. Lily, do you have your cell? Can you call nine-one-one to get help?"

She nodded, flipping her phone out even before I finished my sentence. I grabbed Seth's arm. "We have to go after them. They took off that way. We have to catch them. I think they're going to go through the trees and past that little pond to head the back way to their house.

Then they can get in their car and drive away. We have to catch them!"

Seth was shaking his head. "Jessie, we need to let the police—"

But I was running already, and dragging him along. "No way. No way. It's our school, and he hurt my mom's boyfriend. He's going down."

Seth either changed his mind or gave up, because he started running as fast as I was. We could hear John's feet pounding right behind us. Seth was shaking his head, though. "Jessie, we'll never catch them. They've got a head start, and Mike's the fastest quarterback in the state."

He lowered his voice. "You'd have to use hyperspeed, and there's no way I'm letting you go after them alone."

I'd already thought of that. "I'm not gonna be alone. We're not gonna be on foot."

I skidded to a stop in front of Luke's car. "We're gonna take this. Get in."

John skidded to a stop behind us, almost plowing us over. "Are you nuts? You know how much trouble we can get in, going for a joyride in a sheriff's car?"

I was already opening the driver's-side door. It was my plan, so I was totally driving. Plus, I didn't want to get anybody else in a jam for boosting Luke's car. "It's not a joyride. We're catching the criminals who hurt the sheriff. Now either get in or get out of my way."

Seth climbed in the passenger seat and buckled his seat belt. I grabbed for the keys in the ignition.

Oh, crap. No keys.

I slumped back in the seat. "No keys. Now what do we do?"

Seth held up a key ring. "Looking for these?"

I grabbed them. "But how? Where?"

He grinned. "Under the floor mat on the passenger side. My dad does that, too."

John banged on the wire mesh separating the front seat from where he was seated in the back. "Go, already! Less talking, more driving!"

Then Seth and John both shot totally freaked-out looks at me, and John started yelling. "Oh, no. Driving. And Jessie. Heeeeellllllp!"

I shoved the gearshift in R and backed up fast. *Smash!*

"Don't worry, guys. That was only a small tree. A bush, even," I yelled, as I slammed the car in D and started a massively tight turn so I could head toward the pond on the dirt access road. "Here we go! Hang on!"

The car pounded over that dirt road like some kind of crazy dune buggy. If we hadn't put our seat belts on, I think we'd have shot clear

through the roof of the car on some of the hu-
mongous bumps.

"There they are! You were right, Jess! Right
over there on the side of the pond!"

I sped up till I was almost at the pond and
slammed on the brakes. No way would the car
fit on the skinny path beside the pond. We'd
have to catch them in person.

I shoved the gearshift the two notches to P
and jumped out of the car. "Hold it right there,
guys! We've caught you. You're going to jail!"

Mike and his dad stopped and turned around
to face me. Mike looked totally bummed, but
his dad had an evil sneer on his face. "Shut up,
kid, and stay back, if you know what's good for
you. We don't know what you're talking about,
anyway. We were just out fishing. Right, Mike?"

John and Seth had rushed over to me by then.
Seth kind of growled at Mike. "You even think
about hurting one hair on Jessie's head, and
you'll answer to me, dirtball."

John just stood there, flexing his muscles and
looking mean. "Same goes for me."

Mike looked at his dad, then back at me.
Then he looked at something behind me, and
his eyes got really big, and he started yelling,
"Watch out, Jessie!"

It all seemed to happen in slow motion after
that. Mike jumped across the space between us

and knocked me and Seth sideways. John jumped
on top of us, as though to protect us from Mike.

Then Sheriff Luke's car rolled by us.

But Sheriff Luke wasn't in it.

The four of us stopped wrestling around on
the ground and watched in perfect silence as
the Skyville Sheriff's Department official police
vehicle rolled by us, slowly at first, then picking
up speed.

Right into the pond. *Oops. Guess I didn't push
the gearshift all the way to P.*

Seth broke the silence first. "Wow. I never
knew that pond was so deep."

In less than a minute, all that was left of
Luke's car was the bubbles rising to the surface.
I dropped my head in my hands and moaned.
"This is *so* not the way I planned this."

At my words, Mr. Brooklyn seemed to snap
back from his "watch Jessie drown the sheriff's
car" trance. "Mike. Get over here, and let's go.
We're outta here."

Mike stood up, grabbing my hand and pulling
me up to stand beside him. "No, Dad. I'm staying to face the music. This was wrong, and you
know it. This isn't how I want to get attention.
Not now, not ever."

Mike's dad shook his fist at his son. "You stupid kid. We're rich. The rules don't apply to us.
Now get—"

A voice I hadn't expected to hear for a while broke in. "Actually, the rules *do* apply to you. You're under arrest, Brooklyn. Put your hands out where I can see them. I've still got my gun, and my deputies are on the way, so don't get any ideas, either."

I squealed and ran to hug him. "Sheriff Luke! You're okay! I'm so glad, and you can totally date my mom. You're okay!"

Luke patted my shoulder, then gently nudged me aside. "I'm okay, Jess. We'll talk about the rest of it later. Including the part where you thought playing detective was a good idea. Or the part where you sank my car in the pond."

Oh, yeah. The car-sinking thing.

I'm so dead.

-17-

ALL IS FORGIVEN

"I'm going down. Going to the big house. Gonna wear striped pajamas. Which is so totally wrong, because I look terrible in horizontal stripes. What shoes go with prison outfits, anyway? Do they have prison shoes they make you wear? Am I going to have to wear horizontal stripes and *prison shoes*? Aaarghhhhh!" I rocked back and forth on the narrow bench in the hallway at the sheriff's office, with my arms wrapped around my knees and my head down. My friends were all there with me, lined up in the small space. We couldn't quite see the front door, but were in eye range of Luke's office door, where he was on the phone. Deputies had taken Mike and his dad away twenty minutes ago.

"Jessie. Jessie! Calm down. You're not going to prison," Seth said. He tried to put his arm around me, but I was in no mood for comforting.

I looked up at him. "How do you know? Do you know any good lawyers? Hey, your mom's a lawyer! Will she represent me? I just escaped braces this afternoon, and now I'm going to jail. Why are metal bars suddenly chasing me wherever I go?"

Sniffling back the tears, I looked up at Seth. "Will you call your mom? I get one phone call, right?"

Seth shook his head. "Jessie, Mom's a patent lawyer. She wouldn't have a clue what to do about this. Anyway, Luke's friends with your mom. I doubt he'd put you in jail."

I moaned. "Right. He *used* to be friends with my mom, till I ruined it. Now I drowned his car, too. I'm going to be locked away for the rest of my life."

Lily dropped down on the bench on the other side of me and hugged me. "Jessie, I'll totally bake you a cake with a nail file in it."

I sniffled again and looked at her. "What is that about, anyway? Why is it always a nail file?"

Avielle spoke up from where she leaned against one of the deputys' desks. "Girl, you gotta have a good manicure no matter where you are. We'll put polish in there, and cuticle remover, too."

I dropped my head back down to my knees and moaned again. "Cuticle remover. My life is over."

Just then the front door to the sheriff's office banged open, and I saw Mom come flying in. She never saw us, though, but marched straight into Luke's office and started yelling.

Oh, and when Mom starts yelling—*really* yelling—the walls shake. I grinned a little through my tears.

"*What* have you *done* with my *daughter?* If you think for one minute that I'm going to let you . . . Is she all right? Where is she? Let me tell you right now, *Sheriff,* that I will boot your sorry sheriff butt all over town if you try to do anything, *anything,* that will hurt my daughter. I don't care about your stupid car; I'll buy you a dozen cars. *Where is she?*"

Luke clearly wasn't all that scared of Mom, though—which is kind of unusual—'cause he started laughing.

Which sent Mom over the edge. "Don't you *dare* laugh at me, you . . . you . . ."

I jumped up to run in there before Mom could levitate him right into the next county. I'd never, ever heard her sound this mad.

"Mom! Mom, I'm right here. I'm fine. Don't worry."

Mom swept me into a huge hug and glared at Luke over my shoulder. "Thank God! As for you—"

"As for me," he interrupted gently, "I'd like to thank Jessie for catching the arson perpetrators. And for having the presence of mind to have one of her friends call nine-one-one. And for being brave enough to go after them, although we're going to have to talk about an after-school job at the police station to help pay for the car-sinking damages."

Mom took a deep breath, and I could feel her calming down. Luke stepped out from behind his desk and walked over to us. He hesitated a minute, then he put his arms around both of us and hugged us briefly, then stepped back.

"I'd also like to thank Jessie for telling me it's okay if I date her mom. If the mom in question would be willing, I'd like to take you all to dinner tomorrow night."

Mom looked at me, her mouth falling open.

Then she looked back at Luke and burst into tears.

I grinned at Luke. "I think she's on emotional overload. It's a mom thing."

Seth and Lily and the gang poked their heads in the doorway. "Is everything all right? Is Jessie going to jail?" Lilly asked.

Luke laughed. "Nobody's going to jail. Except maybe Mike and his dad."

The smile faded off my face. "Luke? Mike stepped forward at the last minute. He said he wanted to take responsibility and make it right. Plus, he saved us from being hit by your car. I think his dad kinda made him do it. That should count for something."

Luke nodded. "It will count for something, Jessie. We may ask you kids to testify on his behalf. But for now, I want you to go home. Your parents are on the way. And hear me very clearly: No more playing detective. Got it? You're not the Scooby gang."

We all nodded as we filed out to the hall, where everybody's moms and dads were already pushing in the doors, looking frantic. It was gonna take a lot of explaining, but it was going to be okay. I glanced back at Luke's office and saw Mom smile at Luke before she hurried to catch up with me.

Yep, it's gonna be all right. Oops, one more thing.

I ran back to Luke's office. "Luke? I have to say this all the way through quick, or I'll get all weepy. But here's the thing. You're a great guy, and I'm sorry I was such a creep, and I hope you accept my apology and still go out with Mom, and we can go out for dinner again, and it'll be great, and I can even pay with my savings, and you can order anything you want, except eggplant, 'cause we all know where *that* gets us."

Whew! That was all with one breath.

He grinned at me. "Sounds great, Jessie. I accept your apology, and dinner would be wonderful. But you don't have to pay. And I promise: no eggplant."

I returned his grin and walked back to where Mom was waiting. My mom, who'd put me before anything, even before her feelings for Luke. My mom, who'd acted like a mama wolf when she thought I was in danger.

I hugged her again. "I love you, Mom."

She hugged me back. "I love you too, Jess. But you're still grounded."

Can't win 'em all, right?

Seth, Mom, and Chloe stared at me when I walked in the door of my house on the afternoon of my birthday. But nobody yelled, "Surprise," or "Happy birthday," or anything.

They just stared at me.

So I stared back. (A girl's gotta have a *little* drama, right?)

Mom groaned. Really loud. "Jessie! Well?"

I punched my fists in the air. "I passed!"

Everybody started yelling.

"Woo-hoo!" Seth jumped up off the couch. "I knew it!"

He grabbed me and swung me around the room. Then Mom grabbed me and hugged me. Even Chloe ran up and hugged me, too.

"I'm so happy, Jess," Mom said.

"Me, too, although I was gonna get your room if you had to move out," Chloe said.

"Nice, Stinkerbelle," I said, and reached out to tickle her.

E walked in the house and looked around, smiling. "I assume you heard?"

I ran over and hugged her again, too. "Thank you so much, E. I never could have done it without you. When they turned that hideous shrieky buzzer thing on, I almost didn't notice it after the one you bombarded me with. Yours was much, much worse."

She smiled. "I hoped it was. I thought that way you'd have an easier time with whatever they threw at you. I had trials, too, remember? They did similar nasty noisemaker things to me."

I smiled hugely. "You're the best! You're *all* the best! Now, where's the chocolate fudge cake?"

Mom laughed. "Come on, Mom, Chloe. Come in the kitchen and help me get the cake and ice cream ready. John, Lily, and Avielle should be here any minute."

As they walked out of the room to the kitchen, Seth leaned over to pick up a package from the coffee table. A *present* kind of package.

"For me?" I said, trying to pretend to be surprised.

"For you," he said, handing it to me.

I wanted to be delicate with the wrapping paper, but—hey!—it was a present! I tore into it.

Oooh, it was heavy.

It was bright yellow.

It was another book. . . .

Driving for Dummies.

I stared at it in shock for a heartbeat or two, then started laughing. "Seth, you are a dead man. This had better not be the only present you . . ."

Then I stopped talking, because he was grinning at me and swinging something from his fingers. Something silver and sparkly.

I caught my breath. "Is that . . . ?"

He reached around my neck to fasten the clasp. "It is."

I looked down. There, at the end of the beautifully fragile silver chain, was a tiny red J.

I looked back up at him, speechless.

"It's for Super Jessie. My very own superhero. Happy sweet sixteen, Jess."

Then he kissed me. It was the most perfect birthday *ever*.

SuperJessie@Leagueblog.com

Hello, from your favorite sixteen-year-old superhero! Admit it, I *rock!*☺ I passed every single test, and you were amazed and impressed, I know it!

Well, here I am, back at school and in the real world, all sixteen and everything. Everybody said I wouldn't feel different, but I do. My party was *awesome*. Not just the chocolate cake, but having friends there who cared about me.

Plus, there were presents! Seth gave me the most perfect, gorgeous, beautiful necklace ever! E gave me a pair of kick-butt black leather boots just like hers. Mom and Chloe gave me a gift certificate to the mall, and we're going to have a girls' night out to shop! Yippee!

Plus, listen to this! Sheriff Luke gave me a puppy! Well, it's for me and Chloe both, but I got to name her. I named her Puggsley, 'cause she's a tiny pug puppy and she has the cutest wrinkly face. Chloe and I are taking turns letting her sleep in our room. (Except she has to sleep in her puppy bed, 'cause she still has that piddle problem, but Mom says she'll grow out of that.)

Luke and Mom made up and we had a great dinner out, all four of us. I think he's gonna be a big part of our lives, but that's okay, 'cause he really loves Mom. Plus, he's a good guy. I have a part-time job at the sheriff's office after school two days a week, doing filing and stuff, to help pay for, you know, sinking the car and all. I think I might want to be a sheriff when I grow up, but Luke just shakes his head and moans when I mention it. I don't get what that's about, but grown-ups are weird.

Mr. Platt is back! Well, *my* Mr. Platt. I mean, the old Mr. Platt. But we get to keep the young Mr. Platt, too. He's going to take over driver's ed and teach science, 'cause Snoozebod is retiring soon, and plus the old Mr. Platt doesn't want to do driver's ed anymore. He's not mad at me, either! I brought him some of Mom's fudge cake to apologize about his car, and he wasn't even angry. He said he'd been needing to quit teaching driver's ed for a while, and now he didn't even need to take his nerve pills anymore! Plus, the car company paid to fix his car, 'cause it was under warranty, but they couldn't figure out how the steering wheel could have broken like that.

I just shrugged and changed the subject kinda quick.

So now I'm sort of a hero at school, 'cause I stopped the arson, plus it was pretty much my fault that the young Mr. Platt started working here, and he's such a hottie, so all the girls are happy. It's enormondously awesome to go from zero to hero instead of the other way around, for a change.

Oh! I almost forgot! Thanks for the presents! I mean, thanks even for the books on self-discipline, although you really shouldn't give people lesson kind of gifts. But, still. Thanks! And thanks *hugely* for the hair-straightening ray-gun prototype! It *rocks!* I think I need to be on the development committee, though. I have some cool ideas for different colors and settings and stuff. Don't forget it was my idea when the profits start rolling in, either, okay?☺

Well, gotta go say good-bye to E. She's leaving to go home to her island tonight. I'm gonna miss her, but she said I can come visit for two weeks on my next spring break, all by myself. Mom was a little hinky about it, but I said, "How much trouble can I get into on an island?"

Right?

Super-sixteenly yours,

Jessie

Dear Reader,

Thank you so much for all of your enormously fab letters about how much you loved Jessie and *Super WHAT?* Since that was my very first book for teens, it was totally a relief to find out that you had as much fun with Jessie as I did! I hope you enjoy *Super 16*, too, and write to let me know what you think of Jessie's birthday. Please visit me at my website at www.jaxabbott.com.

Till next time, as Jessie would say: Chicks rule!

Huge hugs,
Jax

Didn't want this book to end?

There's more waiting at **www.smoochya.com**:

Win FREE books and makeup!
Read excerpts from other books!
Chat with the authors!
Horoscopes!
Quizzes!